the moon tells secrets

also by savanna welles

when the night whispers

the moon tells secrets

SAVANNA WELLES

st. martin's griffin
new york

THE MOON TELLS SECRETS.
Copyright © 2015 by Valerie Wilson Wesley. All rights reserved.
Printed in the United States of America. For information, address
St. Martin's Press, 175 Fifth Avenue, New York, N.Y. 10010.

www.stmartins.com

The Library of Congress Cataloging-in-Publication Data
is available upon request.

ISBN 978-1-250-06116-4 (trade paperback)
ISBN 978-1-4668-5419-2 (e-book)

St. Martin's Griffin books may be purchased for educational,
business, or promotional use. For information on bulk purchases,
please contact the Macmillan Corporate and Premium Sales
Department at 1-800-221-7945, extension 5442, or write to
specialmarkets@macmillan.com.

First Edition: March 2015

10 9 8 7 6 5 4 3 2 1

For Faith

acknowledgments

I'd like to thank my agent, Faith Hampton Childs, for her continuing support, encouragement, and most of all, for her friendship. I'd also like to thank Monique Patterson for her editorial support and advice, as well as Holly Blanck and Alexandra Sehulster for their editorial assistance. And to my family; my gratitude for always being there.

the moon tells secrets

navajo skin-walker: the yee naaldlooshii

In some Native American legends, a skin-walker is a person with the supernatural ability to turn into any animal or person he or she desires. . . . Similar lore can be found in cultures throughout the world and is often referred to as shape-shifting by anthropologists.

Some have gained supernatural power by breaking a cultural taboo. In some versions, men or women who have attained the highest level of priesthood are called "pure evil," when they commit the act of killing a member of their family, thus gaining the evil powers that are associated with their kind. It is also believed that they have the ability to steal the "skin" or body of a person.

There is a hesitancy to reveal these stories to those considered "others" or to talk of such frightening things at night.

—excerpted in part from *Wikipedia*

My subject is late. Our appointment was for nine A.M., but an hour has passed and I've heard nothing. A loss of nerve is often the case in matters such as this, particularly when one considers the consequence for betrayal of these "sacred" oaths. I hope the information offered will be worth my time and the fee I've offered to pay and that there will be no objection to my taping our interview.

I am eager—yet strangely wary.

—Denice Henry-Richards
Interview Notes
Recorded April 18, 2011, 10 A.M.
Subject: TKA

1

raine

There are days when I wonder why I was blessed with him—this boy I love with all my heart, who may cost me my soul. I know I must keep him safe from what wants him—wants us—dead, and that the older he gets, the more desperate it will become. Some nights I can't close my eyes for worrying, can't breathe, but then my son will kiss me on my cheek and whisper—*Slow down, Mom, take a breath*—and I'll smile at him, and take that breath like he tells me to. Me, a full-grown woman, listening to an eleven-year-old kid.

I named him Davey for King David, who my granddaddy used to say was twice blessed by God. That was his name, too, and of all the family I knew, I loved him best. Before he died, he taught me how to read and draw and shoot a gun, an old pistol from the war he kept tucked away in his closet. I loved that name, David, the softness of it touched up with strength. But I didn't know how blessed—or cursed—he was when I named him. That came later. His father, Elan, wanted me to name our baby after him, but we'd only been married a year before he died and Davey was born a month after he was gone. I was desperate then. I loved him so much, and I had a newborn son to raise and make as happy as I could—as blessed as I could make him. I couldn't say Elan's name out loud without weeping, and I didn't want to cry those tears on my child.

I can say Elan's name now but still wonder why he left us, even though that isn't the whole truth and I know it. He didn't leave, he was slaughtered, and I know the thing that took him is on its way for Davey, too, and me, because of what my son becomes.

You wouldn't know it if you look at him. He was a pretty baby, is a good-looking boy, and will grow into a handsome teenager. Bright round eyes always on the edge of dreaming, and his Harry Potter glasses make them look bigger. Eyelashes so thick, the Foodtown lady teased him about them last week, that he must be using his mama's mascara—unfair, she said, that a boy should have lashes as pretty as his. He just grinned, the tiny mole just on the side of his lip playing up his wide smile. His hair is black and iron-straight now; Navajo hair he got from his father and Grandmother Anna. He's growing up fast, too fast, and within his boyish body I can see the contours of the man he will become.

His hair was kinky when he was little—curly-kinky like mine and soft around his face like an angel's. My angel with skin as brown and smooth as a Hershey bar. I used to call him that: my Hershey bar with almonds—sweet with little bits of hardness poking through. That edginess will come out the older he gets, Anna warned, the fierceness, viciousness. I didn't believe her, but I do now because I've begun to see it—unlike most of the stuff Anna told me. Usually I just smiled. Anna was as full of lies as she was of love, and half the time I didn't believe what she said. But now I do, since she's been gone; I know now she was telling as much truth as she dared.

She told me early about Davey shifting. Shifting ran through Elan's family, she said, so I'd better get ready, and she'd smile her sly wolf smile, eyes as hard and cold as marbles. Elan must have had it in him, too, what Davey has, but he never showed it—not to me, anyway. It was in her cousin Doba, too, Anna said, who looked so much like her, people mistook them for sisters, but the resemblance ended at temperament. Anna hadn't seen anyone in her family for years, not even Doba, whom she said she'd loved like a sister once. She never told me why she never saw her.

After Davey was born, I lived with my own people, distant family on my father's side, until I got tired of them telling me I was nothing, that the damned baby made too much noise. They were set in their old, ugly ways, used to peace and quiet, and there was too much crying at night, they said, too much giggling in the morning. I moved out after that, to live with Anna, hidden like she was in her red brick house high on top of a hill, high enough so she could take in everything there was to see, be prepared for anyone who might be coming for us.

But the only thing that came for us was Anna, as far as I could tell. I was scared of her that first time I saw her shift and use the gift that Davey has. I decided then that there was nothing I could do but run from her, too, until she found us and brought us back, to keep us safe, she said. And I went because I knew then there was nowhere else I could go, not with Davey being like he was.

And then Anna died, leaving me alone to hide with the money she left, with those last words chasing me wherever I went: *Don't trust nobody. Not family. Not friend. Don't let it get him like it got my son, not until he is ready to meet it. And remember that blood must pay for blood. A debt must be paid. Your boy can never forget. That is his destiny.*

Davey tugged my arm, bringing me back to where we sat in this old church smelling of disinfectant, mold, and incense. The maroon velvet cushions in the pews were faded and ragged, and the pages of the hymn books stacked on rickety shelves so old and torn, they made me wonder how anyone could read them. Yet it was a graceful place—ceilings high and arched, streaks of light glimmering in through red and blue stained glass. No denomination. Probably started out one thing and ended up another. But it was sanctified, sacred space; I could feel that.

"Hey, Raine? What we doing here?" he asked.

"Don't call me Raine," I snapped. I hated for him to call me Raine. It made me feel like he didn't respect me, didn't believe I was really his mother. I was so young when I'd had him, and Anna played mother for so long, taking over our lives, making the tough decisions, paying our way, it made me bitter.

"How come we're here, Raine?" He was stubborn, like his mother.

"Cut it out," I said. "I told you this morning, darlin'."
He didn't like me calling him darlin', any more than I
liked him calling me Raine.

"Mom, please don't call me darlin'! That's embar-
rassing. That's what you call a kid."

"Then don't call me Raine. How many times do I have
to tell you that?" He gave me a half grin. A truce. I edged
over to give a hug, and he eased away. Too old for that, too,
especially in public. "We won't be here much longer. I just
need to go up front and pay my respects, say good-bye."

"To who?"

"My aunt Geneva." But it wasn't just her; it was all of
them—the ones I'd never heard from or known and just
plain forgotten. My mother and father had died when I
was a kid, and my grandparents died after Davey was
born. As far as I knew, Geneva was the only family left
from my mother's side, and now she was gone, too.

"How come you need to say good-bye?"

"Because she's my mother's family."

"Like Mama Anna."

"Like Mama Anna. But from my side, not your daddy's. Her name was Geneva Loving. Like my name was
Raine Loving."

"Didn't Mama Anna have family, too?"

"Some."

"What happened to them?"

"Dead, too, I guess," I said, although I didn't know.

I thought about Doba, remembering how I'd seen her
at Anna's funeral, she and the rest of Anna's family.
There'd been four there, all with that iron-straight hair
and eyes that never left you. Anna's uncle, whose name

no one would say, sniffed around the house like he was smelling for something special until he left, and everybody looked relieved—even Doba, who followed his every move.

When Doba walked into the room, it was like Anna had sat straight up from her casket. Same iron-straight hair, worn brown face, thin fingers that stroked the air like they were tasting it. I'd wondered if Anna's luminous eyes were hidden behind the dark glasses the funeral director gave us so the sun wouldn't hurt our eyes. Doba must have cried as much as me. By then, I'd grown to love Anna like a mother, so I had a space in my heart for Doba, too.

She stared at me and Davey for a long time that day, taking us in like the long-lost relatives we were, made me promise to let her know where we were going so she could stay in touch. Don't want to lose you like I did my cousin, she said. There aren't that many of us left. Just him. She looked in the space where her father had stood, this uncle who had no name. I wondered if they all had the same "gift" as Davey, but I didn't ask. I tried to stay in touch, but not so often as I should have.

"I miss Mama Anna," Davey said.

I nodded and wondered if he saw her in his dreams like I did. Did she whisper warnings like she did sometimes in mine?

Davey suddenly tensed and pulled into himself, but not enough to be dangerous; he only did that when he was scared. Had something frightened him? I studied him closely, looking for the danger signs so we could get out quick. But there were none, just a kid in the loose-fitting Brooklyn Nets sweatshirt he got from Mack, my boss and the owner of Nell's, the restaurant I managed. Davey used to say that Mack was his long-lost grandpa, and Mack would grin when he said it because he felt the same about Davey. Mack taught him to play poker, tie knots, make the chili he was famous for, like my grand-daddy taught me stuff. Nell's was the best job I ever had, the best place me and Davey had ever landed, until a week ago when I knew the thing had found us.

The dog came first, sniffing around Nell's like it had business there, like it was looking for something to eat, slobbering at the mouth with those teeth pointed like they'd been filed, all white and sharp.

"Ain't never seen no hound like that before, hellhound it look like," Jimmy the counterman said when he came back from trying to chase the dog away; he was shivering even though the sun was out. My ears perked up. We'd been here nearly two years and hadn't seen a hint. I'd started believing that Anna was wrong with all her warnings, that we'd finally have some peace from what-ever she claimed was after us. Maybe it had just given up, gone away, left us alone. I pushed Jimmy for more. He'd given the hound some meat, he said, damn thing liked to snap his hand off, tried to run right through him, get its filthy self in Nell's, Jimmy said, and I know Mack wouldn't like that, would he, Rainey? A shiver slid down my back. But I told myself maybe it had just been "a hound," like Jimmy called it.

Until it came back two days later.

Not every part of them makes it when they shift, Anna told me. That's always the way with skin-walkers.

Something doesn't come back like it should, a nose looks like a snout, all wet and thick and nasty; an eye might be bigger than it should be and can't be kept closed, claw tip fingers instead of nails, something will tell you, but you got to see it, Raine, Anna would say, and when you do, take that boy and run for all you're worth. Don't leave a clue behind you.

And that was what I'd always done.

It was in biker guise when it came back again. Must have gotten hold of some poor biker's body and done God knew what with his soul. A red Harley was what it rode, heavy and loud, and the minute I heard it thundering down the road, I knew something was on its way. I watched it climb off the bike, keeping its thick body tight like it was guarding something that might bust out, face hidden by the visor on its helmet. Thick red gloves on its hands, walking on its tiptoes, cautious, like it hurt to move. It slid into a corner table, ordered coffee from Pam, our teenage waitress.

When the school bus dropped Davey off at Nell's that day, it stared at him hard, like it knew him, and said something I couldn't hear. Davey had just shrugged, given that funny halfhearted smile he always gave when he thought I worried too much, then joined me behind the counter. I warned him that night about talking to strangers, and he said he hadn't talked, only nodded, just being polite like I tell him to be. I didn't want to scare him, because I wasn't sure. And it wouldn't make its move right away. Anna had told me that it would play with us like a cat does its prey; it had to be sure the time was right, the night was right. Could be weeks before I saw it again.

But three days passed, and there it was, a dowdy old woman with white-streaked hair; full, pillowy breasts stuffed into a cheap flowered smock; eyes that stared from pink-tinted glasses as it ordered blueberry muffins; paws encased in delicate lacy gloves. I told Davey straightaway when I got home that night we had to go, and all he did was cry.

That didn't surprise me. We'd traveled so much since Anna died, to this town and that, up and down the East Coast from Atlanta to Newark, even up to Boston, then back to Jersey. Wherever we went, he was always the new kid who couldn't say where he'd been. Maybe kids teased him about that or sensed there was something "different" about him; he just never told me. Maybe that was why he cried so hard that night. I cried, too, knowing this was my fault for giving him this life, always running from something, scared to stay in one place long enough. Listening to Anna.

But despite our travels, Davey kept up with school however he could, and after a couple of months he always ended up near the top of his class. He was a reader, like my grandfather was, and he'd read anything you put in front of him—Harry Potter, Percy Jackson—maybe he identified with kids who had a wizard's special edge. Comics he loved, too, and newspapers. Always did his homework—working till it was perfect. But in school he stayed to himself, shy of other kids, because they were shy around him. Yet this place was different. Maybe it was because of Mack helping him feel like he belonged, maybe because we'd managed to stay so long. He'd felt safe enough here to make some friends. Hard-earned friends. Two years was a lifetime for a kid.

"So, Mom, where we going this time?" he said, voice cheerfully fake, his eyes focused on the Spy Mouse app on the Android cell I gave him last Christmas. A sharp pain etched itself into my heart.

"Baltimore."

"Yuck!"

"How can you say that? You've never been there."

"We're not going to be able to take all the stuff we packed, are we? We're going to have to leave most of it behind." He turned off the game and glared at me, lips tight, all pretense of cheerfulness gone.

"We'll take most of it with us."

"Just most?"

"Yeah, most."

"How?"

"We'll rent a truck, okay?"

"Bullshit!"

"Don't curse in church!"

"Don't lie in church!"

"I don't know how we'll take it." I met his glare with my own, and he looked away, unwilling to meet my eyes. "We'll take the important stuff. All your stuff. Maybe we'll rent a car. A van." Mine would fit in a shoe box: photographs of Elan, of Davey as a baby, and of my grandfather David. Valentine cards Elan gave me before he died, birth certificates, mine and Davey's. Davey's stuff filled three of our four suitcases—books, DVDs, video games. Spider-Man toys from when he was three. But it was all important, even if it meant buying new clothes; his "stuff" was his anchor. It had taken him most of yesterday to pack it.

"Promise?"

"We're in church, aren't we?" He nodded. A truce.

The notice in the paper said the viewing would be from nine to ten thirty; we had been here since nine, but nothing was happening. A long oak table stood before an altar covered by rows of lit white candles of various heights. I hoped things would start soon because we needed to be on our way. After this was over, we'd grab something to eat, then get a cab and swing over to the apartment and pick up our things. I'd told the landlord I'd be gone for a couple of days. I didn't give any notice, even though it meant losing my security. I didn't want to risk him mentioning to anybody that we were gone for good.

I looked around the church, suddenly uneasy.

Two others were here besides us. A plumpish woman dressed in white, like a nurse, sat in the front pew. A silk veil as light as gossamer covered her shoulders and her reddish brown cornrowed hair was piled into a loose bun. Her head was bowed as if she were praying. A friend of Aunt Geneva's, waiting like me for things to start, I decided. A man about my age sat next to her. Even from where I sat, I could see he was attractive, his well-toned body nicely filling out his dark business suit. Occasionally, he'd glance at the woman with protective concern, like a preacher does, and I figured that's what he must be.

Davey shifted in his seat, letting me know he was ready to leave. Mack had a brother near Baltimore who'd promised me a job when we got there. Unlike my landlord, I'd given Mack some notice, even though I knew he'd give me a good reference no matter what. I told him not to tell anybody we were moving, and he'd studied my face for answers but promised he wouldn't. I knew he was a man of his word.

We'd take a cab to the bus station as soon as we left the apartment. Despite what I'd said, there would be no van; I was too broke for that. I needed to save every cent until we were settled and I could tell the bank where to send the money that was left from Anna's estate. I glanced at my watch. There was a bus at three; we couldn't stay much longer.

Was it a mistake to have come? We should have gotten up this morning, gone straight to the bus station, and waited in a public space. We could have been halfway to Baltimore by now if I'd done that. But when I saw that name in the obits section of *The Star-Ledger* last night—GENEVA LOVING in big, bold print—I knew I had to come. I needed to hold on to some piece of me that was permanent, that I couldn't toss out like so many parts of my life. Luckily, she'd kept her maiden name, as my mother had, something all the women in my family did. Our tie to ancient roots, my mother used to say before she died.

The name grabbed my attention the moment I saw it. Weren't all that many people named Geneva Loving in the world. Elan used to tease me about that. Raine Loving. Loving Raine. A good name for me, he said, because rain could be soft or hammer hard on a roof but always loving. Nature's way of making things bloom, and that's what I had done for him, he said.

I didn't remember much about Geneva Loving except she could look at your face and tell what you were thinking, and that had made an impression on me. I'd learned to hide my feelings like most folks in my family did, but I couldn't hide from her. How old was I when I saw her that last time? All I could remember was her voice, sweet and tender; it made you feel like something good had just reached out and touched you, and the dim memory of that sound was what had gotten me up and brought us here this morning.

"Stay here," I whispered to Davey. "We'll leave when I come back." Davey was getting restless, as ready to go as I was. Or had something made him uncomfortable? He nodded, a quick motion of his head.

When I got to the altar, the woman rose to greet me. Startled, I backed away, but she grabbed my arm, holding it tightly.

"Thank you for coming. You must be kin. We're about the only ones left, did you know that? I'm Luna," she said, a grin spreading across her freckled face.

"Aunt Geneva's daughter?" I asked, even though her voice and eyes had told me.

"And you must be the reason Mama carried on so about having this memorial, wake, or whatever the heck it is in this old church. Mama never spent a day of her life anywhere near one." She sighed wearily. "But she always knew what she was doing. So we must be cousins. What's your name?"

"Raine." I stiffened, still unsure of her and always wary of strangers.

"'Put it in the paper until somebody comes,' Mama said. I just thought she was going senile. 'Mama,' I told her, 'you know we don't have any family around here,' but she just stared straight ahead, like she always did, and said, 'Post it, baby, just do what I say,' and I did, and here you are."

Luna grabbed me, drawing me into her soft, lush body smelling vaguely of incense, and I let myself go, my whole body taking that breath Davey had told me to take earlier. Yet Anna's warning was still there: Be wary. Be afraid.

"When did Aunt Geneva pass?"

"A week ago. I cremated her like she told me to do, then started putting notices in the paper. I've been coming here every day since."

People had always told me that half my mother's family was crazy and the other mean. I'd grown up with the mean half, and I wondered if I'd found the crazy. That thought made me smile despite myself.

"Don't worry, baby, we're going to just be fine," Luna said, and in that instant I believed her. I wasn't sure why; I just did. "Oh, this is Cade Richards," she added offhandedly, gesturing toward the man standing beside her. "He was kind enough to haul me over here this morning. My old Mustang finally gave out last night. Cade, my cousin Raine."

His smile was shy and took a while to come, but he was as strikingly handsome as he looked when I'd first noticed him, not pretty like some men you see, but good-looking in an old-fashioned, solid kind of way, like Elan had been, like I hoped Davey would be. He struck me as the kind of man who could be leaned on and wouldn't give way, no matter how much baggage you carried. But there was sadness in his eyes; his lips smiled but his eyes didn't. They looked like they hadn't in quite a while.

"Luna's cousin? Nice to meet you." He gave Luna's shoulder a friendly nudge. "You didn't tell me you had family coming." His voice was deep, with a melody to it. It could've belonged to a preacher, but I didn't think so anymore; sexiness like that, preachers learned to hide.

"You're my good friend and neighbor, but you don't know half my business . . . don't want to," Luna said with a saucy wink. There was an inviting ease between them that made me momentarily feel like a member of their circle, and it had been a long time since I was a member of anybody's circle. I was as lonely as Davey, maybe more so. Luna was older than Cade, and I wondered if they were a couple, but their shared glances were more fraternal than romantic—big sister–kid brother rather than older woman–younger man.

"So now I know why I came. It was for you, my dear cousin, and now it's time for us to go." Luna picked up the urn on the altar, planted a kiss gently on the top, and placed it carefully into her oversized tote bag. "Thank you, Mama. As always, you were right, and now I'm taking you home." She gave me a quick grin and added, "We're all going to my new house to send her spirit on its way with turkey sandwiches, tea, and in my case, a Bloody Mary. I'm old enough for that in the middle of the day."

The abruptness of her words and actions puzzled and amused me, and I noticed a glimmer of a smile in Cade's eyes at last. But instantly Luna's expression changed. She lifted her head, as if she heard something in the distance.

"Cade, can you get the car and bring it around so we can get out of here? This tote bag is heavy. Side entrance is good, closer to where you parked. Past time for us to leave," she added, too sweetly. Cade studied her curiously, then nodded and shrugged as if used to following her orders.

"You're coming with us, aren't you, Raine?" she asked as Cade headed out the side exit.

"No, I—"

"Please," Luna said, her eyes pleading so hard, I nodded that I would. We'd stay for a few minutes, then take a cab from there to the apartment, then catch the bus. I searched for Davey in the back of the church but didn't see him. He'd probably gotten bored, ducked down looking for something he'd dropped, his cell phone more than likely; he was always dropping that.

"But we can't stay long." Luna scarcely heard me. Her gaze was focused on someone who had just entered the church.

It was dressed in black this time, from head to toe, a ninja or grim reaper ready for death. It stepped into the room as it had the restaurant, sure of itself, looking around, turning up its dog nose as it sniffed the air, swallowing it, gulping down our scent, and when it saw me, its slanted yellow eyes wouldn't let me go, and its dagger

teeth peeked out from its thick pink gums. I stood staring, unable to move as I watched it stroll away.

How long had it been here? What had it done?

"Davey!" I screamed, finding my voice, tearing myself
from where I stood, running to the back of the church.
"Where are you! Where are you hiding?" I ran to the spot
where I'd left him and dropped to my knees, my heart
pounding. Had it beaten us this time? Had it gotten my
son? I couldn't let myself think, I wouldn't.

"Davey!"

Yet somewhere in my mind, I knew I would sense if
my son was gone. I would know it in my heart. He was
here. I could feel him. Frightened but alive.

"Davey is your son?" I'd forgotten that Luna was behind me.

"He's hiding somewhere," I said, ignoring her question
as I crawled between the pews, stripping out pillows,
searching corners and crevices, my eyes filling with tears
of fear and dread.

And then I saw the glint of his round glasses on the
floor and his clothes—jeans, T-shirt, socks, sneakers—
slipped out of quickly, quietly, left in a pile the way he
did when he got ready for school. And then Davey himself, nestled into a dark corner on the edge of a pew—a
space just big enough for the tiny creature he'd become.
I dropped to my knees, bending down in front of it. "Come
out now. It's okay, Davey. It's okay. It's gone."

He poked his head out first, small, brown, furry, then
eased out the rest: dainty pointed ears and claws; whis-
kers fine as threads; sleek, fast body. Scampering to the

back of the room, he disappeared into a cloakroom. He'd spotted Luna and wouldn't shift in front of her. He never changed in front of me either; that secret he kept with his grandmother, how he made it happen, how long it took.

But this had been a foolish decision, this puny creature he'd become. Easily caught and eaten by the cat, dog, wolf that sought him. A child's choice—quick and small enough to burrow into a tight, hidden space. To disappear without calling attention. Not a wise one. How easily he could have been devoured before I'd know he was gone. Anna had warned me about this. Better to be fierce enough to frighten, she'd always told him. Run and hide until he is big enough, strong enough to fend for himself and for you.

But Anna was gone, and he was just a boy who knew no better. Small creatures were simpler to become than large ones. More his nature. The fierce ones would come later, when he could handle the strength they brought. When he was ready to take blood, to take what was his. Fine for now, she'd told me. Just keep him safe until it's time. And I hadn't.

Church mouse. Squirrel. Bunny. I hadn't gotten a good look this time. All I knew was that I would need to take him home to rest. There would be no leaving town today or even tomorrow. We needed to find a safe place where he could come back into himself.

"You'll stay with me until it's over," Luna said, reading my thoughts as Geneva once had.

I had no choice but to listen.

2

raine

Is it safe here?

There was enough of Anna in me to make me fearful, but this felt like a good place to stay for a day or two. Maybe it was the afternoon sun hitting the pale yellow walls in Luna's living room, bathing them in golden highlights, and the sweet, spicy scent—cinnamon, brown sugar, curry—that floated in from the kitchen. Or the color of the winding stairs, the same shade of turquoise as her tote bag, that led to the second floor, or the battered red and white metal glider swing parked in the middle of her backyard, waiting to be swung in like some relic from the nineteenth century. Or simply Luna herself. But I was able to breathe.

"You all freshen up, and I'll put out some lunch," Luna said as she disappeared into the kitchen, leaving Cade and me standing awkwardly together. I tried not to look at him, but couldn't help myself; his face intrigued me. A square, lightly bearded chin gave it strength, and the lips could be sensual if he gave them half a chance, even though they were now locked in a grimace, tight and unyielding. Something drew me to him, and I hadn't allowed myself to feel that kind of attraction in years. I felt clumsy and graceless standing beside him, as uncomfortable as he clearly was with me. We exchanged forced, stiff smiles, and I noticed again the sorrow in his eyes. I wondered if mine looked that way to him, if my loneliness was so obvious.

Davey was lying on the living room couch. It took him a while to pull back into himself, to pull the inner Davey back from where the outer had been, away from that body, small though it was, that had taken over his own. I could only imagine the movement taking place within him—the shrinking and lengthening and widening, the fear of being seen. I always left him by himself during his transformation, as Anna used to call it. Let him find himself at his own pace. His was an external battle as well as an internal one, taking place where no one could see or hear it.

Cade shifted his gaze to Davey, concern replacing his sadness. "So how you doing?"

Davey glanced up, unwilling, unable to answer. He had buried his face deep into Luna's couch, which was covered in a nubby yellow fabric that looked like sand. Had his mind taken him to the beach, I wondered? Did he remember the feel of the sun and the smell of cotton candy on the Jersey Shore when we dared to escape? Had it all come back just long enough for him to catch his breath and do what he had to do to return? Slowly, he picked up his head, eyes not quite open, staring at me, then Cade.

"Is he okay?" Cade asked, his voice low, and I nodded

he was, although I wasn't sure. It had gotten close this time, closer than it ever had before. I sensed that Davey had known a different, deeper fear.

"He'll be better after he gets some rest."

Davey closed his eyes again, but his breathing had returned to normal.

"What scared him so bad?"

"He just gets scared sometimes," I said defensively, avoiding Cade's eyes. "Panic attacks."

"Panic attacks that severe? In a kid this young?"

"Yeah."

He looked puzzled but didn't pursue it, and I was relieved when Luna bustled into the room with a tray of sandwiches and tea. I was hungrier than I'd thought, but not so hungry as my son, who devoured sandwich after sandwich so quickly, I feared he would choke. Cade watched him, an amused smile on his lips.

"He's definitely better," he said as Davey gulped his tea. Cade picked up the last sandwich on the platter, the only one Davey had left, and gobbled it down himself, then glanced at the door. I wondered if he was married; if there was a wife waiting impatiently for him to return, come home to dinner.

"On your way, of course. Let me get you something to take with you," Luna said, frowning with what looked like frustration as she went back into the kitchen. So there was no one waiting for him. That thought cheered me, and I wasn't sure why.

"Yeah, she's mad at me again," Cade said, embarrassed.

"Luna?"

"Who else?"

"Does she get mad at you often?"

"Ask her." A quick smile that could pass as a smirk flitted across his lips.

"Have you two been friends long?" I took a quick sip of tea, still trying to figure out their relationship.

"A lifetime. What's your son's name?" He tried to change the subject.

"Davey."

"After the king," Davey chimed in from the couch between bites.

"So you know who King David was?"

Davey shrugged. "Guess so. Big-time king. Supposed to be strong, right?"

"Sounds like you know something about history."

"Yeah, but I like other stuff better."

"Like what?"

He was nearly at full strength. The light was back in his eyes, and that brought it back in mine. "Harry Potter, stuff like that."

"Wizards and magic! You sound like the kids in my class."

"So you're a teacher?" I asked.

"Sixth grade. You look about eleven, Davey. You heading to junior high or middle school?"

"He'll be in fifth," I answered for him, defensively.

"Supposed to be in sixth," Davey volunteered bashfully. We'd moved around so much, he was a grade behind.

"Grades don't matter that much. You look like a smart guy to me, that's all that counts." Cade sensed Davey's sensitivity, and I was grateful for that when I saw Davey's grin.

"Yeah, I guess I am sometimes," Davey said, all bashfulness gone.

Luna came back with a brown paper bag, which Cade took, giving her a neat peck on her cheek. With a sigh of exasperation, Luna said nothing.

"So do you two live around here?" he asked, his attention on me.

"We did." Davey threw me an irritable glance.

"Relocating." I stuffed my mouth full of a sandwich so I wouldn't have to explain.

"Well, good luck. Good travels." Cade turned to Davey. "Hey, you know another great writer you should read? Walter Dean Myers. He's one of my favorites. Check out his stuff. You'll like that, too." He gave Davey a quick fist pound. "Take it easy, man, take it slow."

"You, too." Davey's grin made me smile, too. It was good to see this small gesture of male solidarity pass between them; it was something he'd shared with Mack that would be missing from his life now, something that he sorely needed.

"So you like TV?" Luna asked Davey as soon as Cade had gone. "There's one in my bedroom upstairs. Why don't you go up and check out what's on cable. Your mom and I need to talk."

"Can I order a movie?"

"As long as it's not nasty."

Davey rolled his eyes, completely back to himself, and scampered upstairs. Luna settled into the chair next to me, her cup of tea replaced with the Bloody Mary she'd promised herself in church. I knew from the tilt of her head and expression that she was looking for answers, and I owed her that. But she waited awhile before she spoke, stirred her drink, sipped it slowly.

"So why don't you tell me about this son of yours. Why and how often does this happen?"

"What do you—?"

"You know damn well what I mean. I have to know what is going on, because you are in my house—so don't bullshit me."

I had never talked to anyone about Davey before; only Anna knew everything. I searched for words that would make sense, but could find none. I looked away, unable to meet her eyes. Luna grabbed my hand and held it like she was trying to pour her strength into me, and I could almost feel it flowing into my body in sharp, tiny pulses like electricity.

"The telling is always worse than what is told. Begin at the beginning," she said, and I did.

❦

It began when I saw Elan walking down the street that April day, I told her, and me with nothing on my mind except sunlight so strong it made me sweat and dandelions peeking their yellow heads between the sidewalk cracks. I was looking so hard I tripped—and he grabbed me just in time to keep me from falling straight down on my face, his eyes as bright and gentle as Davey's were now, his hands so strong as they held my shoulder. I wanted to tell her about what we had talked about that morning, but I couldn't. Did he mention the broken side-walk? He must have mentioned it, that and how much we both loved the smell of spring. By the end of that walk, longer than we knew it should be, all I knew was that I would see him again.

"From the looks of Davey, he must've been a hand-some man," Luna said.

"He was more than that." I tried to explain how gracious and friendly he was, and how somewhere in that long walk, he'd told me his name meant "friendly," and then, suddenly, I remembered our first date: the movie we could hardly hear because the kids in the front row were doing so much talking, how it rained all the way home, but nothing spoiled it for us, nothing. He was an easy, joyful man, I said, and I loved him more each time I saw him.

"Sounds too good to be true, but true love always is," said Luna.

"But there was always fear, apprehension in his eyes that I never understood until I had his child. He didn't talk much about his family, just that he was half black, half Navajo, and an only child like me. We were loners, the two of us, bound together the moment I touched his hand. Long before we married, we had taken our vows with our souls."

"And then came Davey?"

"Quickly. And I met his mother, Anna."

"What was she like?"

"There was a wariness about her, too, as if she were afraid of me and the baby, and when she touched my womb, bending down to listen like she could hear the baby's heartbeat, it frightened me. Her love was so fierce, it went straight through to the baby. I was sure of that. I didn't tell *our* people I was married and pregnant; I didn't want their sourness to touch the sweetness in my life."

Luna chuckled. "Some of our kin could definitely take the sweetness out of life. I'll tell you that. Geneva had her sweetness, but sourness was all she got back—from our folks, and from her husband. My father."

"You have sweetness, too, Luna," I said, finally letting go of her hand.

"I have my moments."

"I was eight months pregnant when he died." I looked away, not wanting Luna to see the tears that came into my eyes even after all these years.

"How?"

"Murdered."

"And the murderer?"

"Never found him."

I avoided Luna's eyes because I didn't want to talk about that day, about what was left and torn up so bad I didn't recognize him. It had ripped him inside out, taking every part of him I loved, everything I cherished. I nearly lost Davey the day I found Elan, thrown against the wall in the garage where he'd parked the car. Anna had come there, too, found me on the floor, hadn't uttered a sound, just called two men I'd never seen before to help her bury him someplace in the dark inside her land. She'd said no more about it except that it had gotten her son and it would come for mine.

I couldn't tell all that to Luna, so I went back to what she had first asked me.

"Davey has a gift, Luna. He changes when he needs to become something else."

"Changes? What do you mean?" She tightened her gaze on my face, as if she could find out what lived behind it.

"His body changes. His mind. He can turn himself into anything he wants to be. It's small animals now, a mouse, a squirrel. But later it will be different. A wolf. Another person."

Luna caught her breath, then let it out; she hadn't meant for me to hear it. "What do you mean turn himself into another person?"

"He can't do that now!"

"What do you mean?" she asked again, demanding to know.

"Take somebody's body. Snatch somebody's soul."

She took a long, lazy swallow of her Bloody Mary. "His father, Elan, had it, too, this . . . gift?"

I thought about our family and the boon, they used to call it, that some of us were supposed to have, the one I missed, the one they said Geneva had; Luna must have gotten it, too, her "gift." "I think he did, but he never told me. Anna had it. I know that. She never talked much about her side of the family. Just her cousin Doba, and an uncle, who Anna said was evil, who had done something that pushed him from the family."

"So what did Davey see in church?"

"The same thing you saw, Luna. The thing that left. It was what killed Elan, the murderer they never found, because they couldn't. It's looking for us now. Davey more than me."

Luna took another swig of her drink, then put it down on the coffee table, carefully mopping the ring the glass left with a Kleenex drawn from her bosom. "Best place to store them if you got as much as I do," she said, pushing it back down between her ample breasts. "And what is this *thing*?"

I paused, not sure how much to tell her. There were so many things that were secret, vows Anna had taken, that she'd made Davey take, that couldn't be told outside the family.

"I just know what Anna told me—that it killed Elan and it would not rest until it killed Davey, too, because of the gift. He has what it wants. It can't live and let him live, too. Its time is coming to an end."

"Like an old wolf or lion in a pride?"

"I don't know. All I know is that it or they are evil beings, Luna, and Davey has that in him, too."

Luna smiled. "There's nothing evil about your boy."

"Anna said there would be someday, when it comes out in him."

"I've run into my share of demons, Raine, and there's no demon in him. I don't know about the thing that you say is chasing you. I only got a glimpse of it."

Luna kept her thoughts to herself as she collected what was left over from the lunch, and after a moment or two she asked what we wanted for dinner. I told her I wasn't hungry but if she had any more sandwiches, Davey would probably like some, and she said she could do better than that. She went upstairs to check on Davey; he'd fallen asleep.

"Whatever he goes through takes a lot out of him,

and you, too. Why don't you go upstairs and lie down beside him. I'll make up the bed in the guest room where you and he can stay tonight. It has a trundle bed you can pull out for now, and then, when he's ready, we can put him in another room. This old house is bigger than it looks. We can get your things later."

"I don't know. . . ." I wasn't sure how long we could stay.

"Whatever that boy has after him it won't stop until it tries to kill him, because it knows the child will someday have the power to destroy it. It has to get him while he's young."

"Anna told me that," I said.

"Did she tell you that you can't take down evil without a fight, a good fight?"

"No, Anna said—"

"You've got to stand your ground, Raine. Or you'll be running for the rest of your life. You may keep him safe, but you'll cripple him while you're doing it, and you don't want that kind of life for Davey, do you?"

Had I been selfish, weakening him with too much protection? I'd never thought of it like that.

"In the meantime, you should try to bring some normalcy into the boy's world. I heard you say Davey's a grade behind in school. Cade's a teacher—maybe he can tutor him over the next few weeks until we figure something out."

I was too tired to argue, but I knew what I would do regardless: We'd stay here for a couple of days, to make Luna feel better, then be on our way like we always were, like Anna said we should be.

So I went upstairs and the next thing I knew, Luna was calling us down for dinner: cream of chicken soup and toasted whole wheat bread she'd made the day before. Healthy food, she said, something we both needed. And I settled in that night, with Davey in the trundle bed beside me, the soft blue color of the walls drawing me into them.

"Mom," Davey whispered after a few minutes, surprising me because I'd thought he was asleep.

"Yeah, son."

"I won't be small like that again, like I was in church today. Never. I'm through with it."

"Okay," I said. "Try to go to sleep." I leaned over and pulled the cover up to Davey's shoulders, and he shook it off, his reminder that he wasn't a kid anymore, and soon the stillness of the room and the sound of my son's breathing sent me to sleep.

At daybreak, something woke me, pawing at Luna's gate outside, and there was a howl—low and deep like a dog. But it could have been just about anything, I told myself. A stray dog trying to come in from the cold or Pinto, Luna's gray poodle, locked outside crying to come into the house. And I was tired and strangely peaceful, so I drifted back to sleep anyway, lulled by the sound of the electric fan whirling on the top of the bureau.

3

cade

"Dennie."

Cade whispered his dead wife's name, and that brought fleeting comfort as had the lilacs he cut earlier that morning. He'd buried his face in the blossoms, leaving a trail of tiny purple flowers trailing behind him when he carried them into the house. How long had they been blooming? Dennie would stuff green branches of new lilacs into the square glass vase on the dining room table. "Officially spring," she would always say, and so it was.

It was evening now. He sat across the table from where she'd once sat, books, pencils, and papers piled high and messy around her. He stared at the lilacs for as long as he could stand it, then dumped vase, flowers, and water into the trash can in the kitchen. It had been a year since her death, and nothing could dim his grief. Nothing would bring her back.

Six months ago, he'd put the house on the market, thinking that would make it easier for him to "move on," as all the teachers at his school suggested. Better not to be reminded every moment each day of what he had lost, they advised. It would be a quick sale, the Realtor assured, this charming three-bedroom house with its brand-new kitchen, shiny floors, and wood-burning fireplace. But when potential buyers got wind of what had happened in the first-floor office, now neatly painted a cheerful daffodil yellow, they hauled ass away as fast as they could; the damned house could not be sold. Moving on was as impossible as moving out.

He pulled a bottle of Jim Beam, one of the three that lined the shelf in his kitchen cabinet, and poured himself a generous shot. Glass and bottle in hand, he settled down on the plush leather couch in front of the TV and downed its contents, enjoying the sting of golden liquid as it rushed down his throat into his belly.

He hadn't been in a church since Dennie's funeral. If he'd known that was where Luna was headed this morning, he would have found a way to get out of it, except that Luna, bless her soul, would have known he was lying and called him on it. It amazed him how close they had become since Dennie's death. She'd turned into the big sister he always wanted, the dependable buddy he never had. It was a good thing, too. If it hadn't been for Luna Loving Moore, he would have drunk himself to death by now or jumped off a bridge or taken that useless gun left on the office floor that night and blown a hole through his mouth. Damned, stupid gun, for all the good it did Dennie. For all the good it did.

He squeezed his eyes closed to blot out what he never wanted to see again: her face ripped off—that darling, square chin and luscious lips that never stopped smiling;

her copper-colored skin torn from the bone; short, natural hair ripped from its roots. Her body gutted, the way his father used to gut the deer he butchered, insides spread out in ropes of red and brown and yellow on the rug, a butcher's killing floor. And her eyes, which had shone so brightly once, he swore she could see at night— like a cat, he would tease her, and she would scold him because she hated cats. I'm a dog person, she would say, and that was what he'd planned to get her for her birthday, a beagle puppy because she liked Snoopy.

Where were her eyes? Where had they gone? What had they done with them?

Luna had found him that night, whimpering and nearly unconscious. She covered what was left of Dennie with a pink sheet found in the hall closet on the second floor, then grabbed and held him until the cops came, his broken, jagged sobs shaking her body as violently as they did his own. The police eyed him suspiciously at first, questioning him relentlessly about what had happened in that room until the coroner explained that Dennie—the deceased—had been killed early that afternoon. Cade had been in school all that day. Yet there were no signs of a break-in. Burglars probably, the cops suggested, crazy men high on drugs like crystal meth. The door must have been unlocked, the cops said, and they had surprised her. It had had to be more than one; that was a given.

But why kill her like that, tear her apart so brutally? they asked among themselves even as Cade stood listening. They sought clues but found nothing—except the smell. Luna, sniffing the air upon entering, had slapped her hands over her mouth and nose, as if protecting herself from some unspeakable threat. Cade had caught a whiff of it, too, an animal odor that belonged in the woods, and he knew that because when his father would hunt, he would sniff the air as Luna had, determining what wildlife was about. His father was long dead, and Cade hadn't hunted with him since he was a kid, but he remembered how he sorted the air for that smell—even his grief hadn't overpowered that memory.

My God, how he had loved her. Luna had loved her, too.

Dennie had been the only neighbor in the decidedly upwardly striving working-class neighborhood to befriend the odd-looking woman often dressed in white flowing dresses who smelled of exotic spices and who more often than not pulled Pinto, her yelping poodle, on a rope behind her. He was a strange looking creature; about ten inches tall with thick, messy gray fur. His owner obviously balked at giving him a conventional poodle cut, so he looked and moved like an oversized puff of dust. Cade felt like an outsider when he'd come home from school that first afternoon and found Luna and Dennie giggling like schoolgirls as they sipped tea and swapped herbal remedies.

"Luna Moore is an old soul," Dennie said meditatively after their neighbor left. "She actually understands the stuff I'm writing about."

"That voodoo stuff?" He'd raised his eyebrow as he always did when it came to his wife's research.

"Not voodoo, Vodun—and that is a valid belief system if you know what you're talking about—but I'm not talking Vodun. I'm talking Navajo not Haitian, mythology not religion."

"I thought Jersey was Lenape territory. Don't Navajos live in the Southwest?"

"But some of the myths and beliefs are similar. There are clusters of Navajo people around here, too. They're like black folks with our diasporas, intermarriages, mythical beasts coming together where you least expect to find them."

"It's all witchcraft, as far as I'm concerned," he'd said with mock gruffness. "And I don't believe in witches."

Dennie continued sorting through a pile of papers. "You would if you read the stuff I've read."

He'd grinned and let it go. Years of listening to his wife explain the passion that led her to seek a doctorate in cultural anthropology had left him charmed, curious, and finally, a bit bored. That stuff is over the head of a fifth-grade teacher, he'd joke. Study something I can get, like the cultural life of the typical eleven-year-old. I'll wait for my own kid to study that, she'd say, and they'd shared the grin they always did and he'd gone back to correcting papers and she to the myths that fascinated yet haunted her. Kids would come in time, they'd long ago decided. After she'd done her research, after she wrote her dissertation, after she got a job. They had the rest of their lives, after all.

"So you've found a fellow traveler in Luna Moore? I knew there was something weird about that woman," he'd said in bed that night.

"Not weird . . . just wondering. She doesn't dismiss unexplainable things like some people do." She'd given him an affectionate kick. But he'd still regarded Luna with a wary eye.

All that had changed.

He poured himself two shots of bourbon, perused the papers he had to correct, and pushed them aside. He'd do it Sunday night, put off watching the playoffs, get to school early on Monday. Weekends were the hardest. He focused on the kids during the week; thirty eleven-year-olds were enough to keep anyone on his toes. Their silliness, misbehavior, and occasional pranks kept him from going crazy. The kids and Luna.

He wondered again about the boy with Luna's cousin. Funny how shy and shaken he was at the house, as if all his energy had been zapped away, like something had left him scared down to his roots. Something strange about the woman, too. Not surprising they were kin to Luna, Queen of the Odd. What was the woman's name? Rene? Lane? Raine.

Luna didn't mention family much, and he'd been surprised when she told him her mother had died and asked if he'd accompany her to the memorial. It was foolish of him not to have realized they'd be going to a church. But she'd been so vague about the service, and it really could have been held anywhere—knowing Luna. He'd expected some kind of ceremony, but they'd simply sat in the front pew as if waiting for mourners to show up, and finally someone had: the boy and . . . Raine. Pretty name, pretty woman.

Only recently had he begun to notice women again. He'd assumed that anyone he found attractive would look like Dennie. Raine was different. She was taller than Dennie by a foot and thinner, with skin as brown and smooth as maple syrup and a bunch of wild, springy curls that bounced around her face like a wayward halo. There was a wariness about her, as if she needed protection—nothing like Dennie, who wasn't afraid of anything. If only she had been afraid, more careful, cautious.

A deep ache swelled inside him, as that night came back.

Denice, what you doing? Friday, their night for red wine and pasta. He'd found a good bottle of Chianti, bought two because he knew she would like it, and they could drink it the next night, too. *Hey, Den, you home?* He'd put the groceries on the kitchen table, nearly dropping one of the bottles, cursing to himself. *Denice!* He'd yelled, not knowing then that he would never again say her name except in sorrow. The silence in the house had been utter, profound.

The door to her study was open, which surprised him; she always kept it closed. For an instant, his mind couldn't make sense of what he saw—the smear of red that surrounded her; the smell that was there, then wasn't. What was she doing with red paint? had been his first thought. Funny how your eyes could take in just pieces of horror, as if your mind couldn't conceive the whole and still be sane. He'd seen the gun then, her father's gun she kept in her office drawer. It lay next to her, just beyond her reach. And then her face, what was left of it. Had he screamed? He must have; he couldn't remember.

The phone ringing in the kitchen pulled him back

from that night, and he let it ring for a minute so he could get his bearings. He knew who it was; nobody else called him.

"Did you eat yet, or are you just sitting there drinking scotch?" said Luna on the other end. He put the glass down on the kitchen counter and pulled a sandwich out of the bag she had packed for him.

"Bourbon, not scotch. I've always hated scotch because my dad drank it, and I'm eating now." Dutifully, he took a bite of turkey sandwich and it turned dry in his mouth; he forced himself to chew.

"You should have stayed here longer. Ate with me, Raine, and the boy, like somebody with good sense."

The sandwich stuck like paste to the roof of his mouth and he took a swig of liquor to chase it down. "I don't have good sense, Luna, don't you know that by now? And I had work to do. I'm not fit company for normal people, anyway, particularly a kid."

"I'll let those lies lay where they landed. You have good sense, and we both know you had nothing better to do. You're good with kids. You're a teacher, for crying out loud."

"I have a defined role there. And they need me."

"This boy might have needed you, too, for all you know." Cade shrugged, not bothering to answer. "You never know who needs you and who doesn't. But I do know one thing, *you* could have used the company."

"Did you mention—?"

"No. I'll leave that to you."

"What makes you think—?"

"Don't let what took Dennie devour you, too," Luna

said, cutting him off. "Throw that gin, bourbon, or whatever the hell you're drinking down the sink and brew yourself a cup of coffee."

She hung up without waiting for an answer. Cade listened to the silence for a moment, then placed the phone facedown on the counter. He knew she would call back in a minute to apologize, but he didn't want to talk anymore. He went back into the living room, watched a few moments of ESPN, picked up the remote to channel surf, turned off the TV, and stared at the blank screen. Maybe he should have stayed at Luna's. Made small talk. He'd been good at that once. He'd been a rational man—charming, he'd been told—with his feet squarely planted in the here and now.

I only believe what I can see, hear, taste, touch, or smell, he'd said to Dennie on their first date. There's so much more to life than you can touch, see, feel, taste, or smell, she'd told him, licking candy sprinkles off a cone of vanilla ice cream. You can taste, smell, feel, see this ice cream. What more do you want from life? he'd said. Maybe the essence of cold, sweet, and vanilla. The *reality* of things, Dennie replied.

But there were realities he didn't want to understand. The reality of fear, for one thing, that made it impossible for him to think; of terror that crept through him when he wasn't expecting it; and smell, the one that made Luna slap her hand all over her face that night. Was he imagining it, or was it back now, just for an instant? He sniffed the air, held his breath.

He was drunker than he'd thought, nearly toppling over when he tried to stand. Hard liquor had never been his thing, because that was what his father used to drown things out—scotch, vodka, gin. Never bourbon. A half smile spread on his lips as he thought about his old man. Yeah, maybe he'd been too hard on him, maybe that was exactly where he was supposed to end up—a functional alcoholic like his father had been. For all he knew, his father had seen something, too, something beyond reason that had forced his head inside out and then into a bottle.

Don't let what took Dennie devour you, too.

It already has, he said aloud.

Willing himself straight, he made his way to the kitchen and poured the liquor in his glass down the kitchen sink. Then, without thinking hard about it, he went into the room where he'd been only twice since Dennie's death.

There would be no trace of what had happened, thanks to the professional cleaning service, recommended by the cops. Dennie's office was as clean and neat as it had been when she was alive. He walked across the room, pulled up the shades, and opened the window to let in the evening air. A cool wind drifted inside and he stood, enjoying the coolness on his face. Pulling the overstuffed office chair away from the desk, he settled into it, snapped on the desk light, and began to study the things she'd left behind: papers stacked in rows; pencils, pens, and markers in the china mug she'd won at Great Adventure; a yellow-checkered soup bowl filled with pink paper clips and Post-its. Her favorite wedding photograph, Dennie in a neat, stylish white suit—she was not one who believed in satin wedding gowns—lay facedown on the desk next to the folders. He hadn't been able to look at it for months, but he did now, staring full into her face until his eyes watered. He placed it back, careful to sit it at the angle where she'd had it. The digital recorder she used for notes and interviews was here somewhere, but he couldn't bring himself to look for it. He sure wasn't ready for that yet, to hear the sound of that voice always bubbling with mirth and wonder, the laughter that rode the end of every word. No, not that. Not for years, he was sure of that, not until he was on his deathbed and knew he would join her soon. Then maybe he'd play them once, before he saw her again in kingdom come.

What should be done with everything, all these recordings and the pages marked with notes and variously colored Post-its? Matt Wilson, Dennie's advisor, had called several times to offer his condolences and remind him what a brilliant young researcher she had been (as if he didn't know) and how vital her research could be in the field. He'd offered to go through her papers and the recorded notes she left, to see if there were things that might be useful to other students. Cade had flatly refused. It was too soon, he'd said. He wanted to go through everything himself.

Yet he had no idea where to start or what she had been working on. He picked up one of the folders, read the first few paragraphs, and could make no sense of it. Why hadn't he just let the man come and take what he wanted? Even as he asked the question, he knew the answer: It had just been too much. Too much to think about, too much to do. But a year had passed—maybe it was time to let whoever wanted it, have it.

He opened the drawer where he'd stuffed the manila envelope filled with objects the police returned after having taken them that night. Some thoughtful soul had separated Dennie's wedding ring from the rest of the "evidence" and given it to him when he'd gone by the precinct; he wore it now on a chain around his neck. He didn't care much about anything else, hadn't even wanted to look.

There wasn't that much here anyway: her father's old .38; gold cross that had belonged to her mother; silver ankle bracelet she seldom wore; tiny painted drum; three silver bullets; what looked like a piece of a claw—he couldn't tell which kind, only that it was yellowed, like aged ivory, and about five inches long and an inch or so in circumference. An eagle's talon? It was longer, heavier than they usually were.

Why had she kept it? She'd shared all her strange "artifacts," as she called them, with him. He'd seen the bullets more than once. (Five silver bullets should be enough to kill anything that growls in the dark. They sure cost me a pretty penny, she'd joked.) And the drum a month before she died. Was this one for luck, this . . . appendage? The tip was stained with what looked like blood, and that made him uneasy. Better not to look too closely, he thought, stuffing it back where he'd found it. Maybe Luna would know why Dennie had kept it. She knew about stuff like that.

The phone rang and a smile crossed his lips. Just think about the woman and she calls, he said to himself as he went into the kitchen to answer it.

"Wanted to check on you, and to apologize for hanging up on you like I did. The last thing you need from me is attitude."

As if Luna could see it, Cade guiltily placed the bottle of Jim Beam sitting on the counter back into the cabinet. "Forget about it, Lu. I'm used to your attitude by now, but listen, I found something . . . kind of weird . . . with the stuff the cops brought back. It looks like some kind of a talisman or something. Did she mention anything like that to you?"

"So you're finally going through Dennie's stuff. What brought that on?"

"I don't know. I just felt like it. But not all of it. I'm not ready for that yet."

"What kind of talisman?"

"I don't know, like an old finger, part of a claw. Weird."

"That doesn't sound like a charm to me. Where is it now?"

"Back in the drawer with the rest of the stuff. I don't like looking at it," he said, and to his surprise, he shuddered.

"What scares you about it?"

"I didn't say that," he said, too forcefully.

"I want to see it."

"Maybe I should just throw it—"

"No," Luna interrupted him. "Drop it in a bag and keep it in another room."

Cade chuckled. "Luna. That sounds like something Dennie . . ." He stopped midsentence, unable to finish.

"You okay?"

"Yeah."

"Maybe that is a little extreme."

"Very extreme."

"Is it okay if we drop by tomorrow—me, Raine, and the boy? I'll check it out then. And something else, Raine might have a . . . well, a proposition for you."

"Proposition?" What was that about?

"Just something you can help her out with. Her and the boy. After breakfast. And try to get a good night's sleep."

Cade laughed out loud when he heard that, bitterly. Luna, silent on the other end, knew as well as he that a good night's sleep was gone to him forever.

4

raine

The theme song from *SpongeBob SquarePants* jerked me awake. Davey, in one of his playful, mischievous moods, must have programmed it into my cell. I switched it off, annoyed but amused. Early morning light poured into the window and my heart beat fast until the soft blue color of the walls in Luna's house, and the clean, crisp feel of her guest sheets against my bare skin, called me back, soothing me. I took one of Davey's breaths—in slow, out easy—and glanced at the screen to see who had called me. It was Mack, my old boss.

I knew what he wanted, to check and make sure I'd made it to Baltimore okay, if I'd gotten that job he told me about. In the two years I worked for him, I'd gotten used to his protection, always looking out for me—calling when I was late, handing out advances on my salary when I was broke, saving the best cuts of steak every now and then for me to take home for dinner. And even more for Davey. When there was money needed for some special project at school, Mack was the one who dug out his wallet and slipped a twenty into Davey's pocket.

Money needed for the class trip? Mack was there, no questions asked. Guilt shot through me. Despite everything he'd done, I never really trusted him—not even after two years. I'd never let him know what was really going on in my life, what was after us.

Trust no one. No one.

Anna's voice pushed into my mind as it always did, and I turned off the phone without answering. I'd call him later. I needed to let him know we were okay, tell him how he could reach us if he needed to—for Davey as much as for me. I couldn't just let him disappear from my life, as I had so many other people we met in our traveling. Just keep moving, never look back, Anna had said, but that didn't apply to Mack. I wouldn't let it.

You don't want that kind of life for Davey, do you?

No!

I'd answered Luna's question the moment she asked it.

Then I remembered the sound I'd heard last night, the scratching on wood somewhere I couldn't see, and my gaze drifted to Davey still asleep on the trundle bed beside me, his long eyelashes nearly touching his cheeks. My angel. He wouldn't want to hear that, tough as he thought he was, and my breath got tight again as I thought of how close we'd come in that church. How vulnerable he had been. Not tough at all, just scared and tiny.

I won't be small like that again, like I was in church today. Never. I'm through with it.

How could I keep him safe?

Until we figure something out.

Davey must have felt my gaze because he opened his

eyes, one at a time like he does when I try to get him up for school, then he squinted like he was scolding me.

"Your crazy phone woke me up," he said, just this side of fresh.

"My crazy phone!"

"Who called this early?" Both eyes were open now, and there was alarm in his voice even though he tried to hide it.

"Mack. I'll call him later. And take that foolishness off my phone."

He chuckled as he headed down the hall to the bathroom. I heard Luna downstairs in the kitchen, cooking, humming to herself, and by the time I'd made our beds, the smell of bacon, biscuits, and coffee drifted upstairs. I savored the normalcy.

By ten, the three of us had eaten, dressed, and were standing in front of Cade's front door. Much to Davey's delight, he and Pinto had become fast friends after Davey snuck him several of Luna's biscuits. As we stood on the porch, he tried to jump into Davey's arms and when Davey picked him up licked his face. "Bad dog," he scolded, giggling as he grabbed and held him tight.

It took Cade a while to answer the door, and when he did, I wondered if Luna had told him we were coming. The kitchen was a mess. Plates and glasses were piled high in the sink, and a frying pan caked with grease sat on a burner of the stove. The room smelled like burned bacon and scorched toast. Yet there were hints that it had once been different and decorated with care: white oak cabinets, rose-colored walls, and sheer white curtains gave the room a dainty touch, but whoever she was had come and gone. Cade, in torn jeans and a wrinkled red T-shirt, looked half-sleep.

"Hey, come on in, want some coffee?" He beckoned us into the kitchen as he wiped his mouth with a napkin. His sneakers were unlaced. I squelched the impulse to suggest he tie them.

"Sure it's okay?" I asked instead.

"No, it's fine. Mornings start a little late for me some days." He glanced at Luna, who rolled her eyes.

"Davey, there's a backyard for you and Pinto to play in if you want. He needs to run," she said, plainly clearing the way for me and Cade to talk. "I want to see that thing you mentioned last night," she said to Cade, and a look passed between them I wasn't meant to see. Cade gave a nod toward the back of the house, and Luna, tote bag in hand, headed down the hall. His face filled with a quick anguish that Davey saw, too. He began to nervously bounce Pinto's ball, and the rhythm of the rubber hitting the linoleum momentarily broke the tension. Distracted, Cade picked up a sponge and swiped the table in long, methodic swipes.

"Go on, Davey," I said. Without looking at either of us, he headed outside, Pinto trotting eagerly behind him.

I sat down at the table and Cade tossed the sponge across the room into the sink, basketball-in-hoop style like a kid would, then sat down across from me.

"Luna said something about a proposition you have for me?" He got right to the point.

"Proposition?" The word, conjuring up images of seduction and steamy sex, was not the one I would have used. "I hope you won't be disappointed!" I added without

52

thinking how it sounded, something I rarely do, but it made him smile, a shy, good-natured smile that lit up his face, and the room seemed lighter, too, a complement to the pink walls and pretty white curtains.

"Depends on what it is?" he said, playful smile still on his lips, and I realized how easy it would be to flirt with a man like him, something I hadn't done with any man since Elan's death.

"Well, I wanted to know if you'd tutor my son over the summer. If you have the time," I quickly added, suppressing any coquettish urge I had. "Maybe shorter. A few weeks, maybe." A few days. Just enough time to satisfy Luna.

"Summer or a few weeks? There's a big difference."

"I'm not sure yet." He hesitated, looking doubtful, and I added, "I can pay you."

"It's not the money."

"Listen, it's okay—"

"Sure," he said before I could finish. "School's over in a week and I don't have much else to do. Yeah, I'll do it."

"He's easy to teach, eager to learn and—"

"I know. I can tell he's a nice kid."

"Thanks. For teaching and for saying that."

"Don't thank me too soon. You need to be honest with me, tell me more about him, about what's going on."

"Like what?" I was defensive, hearing the edge in my own voice. It was there because it had to be. It surprised Cade, too, I could tell that, but his eyes and voice softened.

"Like what you want me to teach him, for one thing.

Like why you don't know if it will be the summer or a few weeks. Like what dreams you have for him."

"My dreams for him? I don't know. Whatever he wants for himself. If you could just help him catch up with what you were doing this year so when we move he can be in the grade he's supposed to be in," I said, ignoring the second question.

"So you're definitely relocating like you said last night?"

"Yeah, probably." I studied the streaks the sponge had left on the table because I didn't want my eyes to meet his. "I'm not exactly sure when—a few weeks, maybe."

"Or the end of the summer." He shifted his gaze away then back to me. "Raine, you'll forgive me for asking you this, like I know I just met you, but are you running away from someone? Like Davey's father, maybe?" I heard in his voice what the kids in school must have heard when they were scared or in trouble, and what whomever he had shared this house with had probably seen when he held her close. I felt like one of those kids, wondered how it would be to unburden myself to someone with such tenderness in his eyes. I thought about Elan, then made myself stop.

"Davey's father is dead. I'm a widow. Davey's father died shortly before he was born," I said quickly, hoping that would be enough. He went to the counter and poured a cup of coffee, nodded at me, asking if I'd like some, too, and I told him I would. "So how long have you known Luna?" I changed the subject; I didn't want to tell him anything else, let those thoughtful eyes pull anything out of me.

"About a year and a half. She and Dennie . . ." He

began again. "She and my late wife, Denice, were good friends. So I guess you've known Luna all your life." He took a swallow of coffee; he was changing the subject, too.

"No, I just met her."

"You're not serious?" he said, sitting back down.

"Yeah, actually I am." The coffee was hot and bitter. I like mine sweet, half filled with milk. Two teaspoons of sugar, three when I'm by myself. He must have noticed my distaste.

"Forgot to ask, want some milk? I take mine black. I'm out of sugar. Got some honey, though." He took a carton of milk out of the refrigerator and placed it in front of me.

"This is fine." I'd picked up the whiff of sour milk when he put the carton on the table.

"But then how did she know that you were coming? I couldn't believe it. It was like she was waiting for you," he asked, getting back to Luna.

"Let's just say my family has a sense of things to come. I'll leave it at that."

"And do you have a sense of things to come, too?" He was obviously curious; I almost hated to disappoint him.

"No. Mostly I try to believe in the here and now, what I can see, hear, feel, or touch." I was lying and wondered if he knew it. I didn't understand what was chasing us or why Davey was the way he was. There was no such thing as the here and now.

"Mostly?" he said with a hint of amusement touched with something I couldn't identify, but he didn't ask me to explain, so I didn't.

Davey came in then, Pinto yelping at his heels. Seeing the two of them together like that, suddenly old
friends, made me grin. Ever since he was old enough to
see the "ideal" family on TV—mom, dad, two kids, family dog—he had yearned for a pet—dog, cat, guinea pig,
anything—since the dad and two kids thing was obviously off the table. He'd begged me so often for a pet,
I'd actually thought about giving in, and then I'd think
about our reality and know it couldn't work. Traveling
around too much, I used to tell him. It's hard to keep a
dog in an apartment. But there was something else, darker,
that I didn't ever say, and when he got old enough to
understand, he stopped bringing it up altogether. Animals were a threat to him. Even small ones. A pet might
see him as prey or become *his* victim.

"Did you all have a good time out there?" I asked, and
Davey nodded.

"He likes to catch. He's kind of old, but he still likes
to do it." He rolled the ball to Pinto, who, as frail as he
was, managed to catch it. Not a perfect playmate, but
close enough for now.

Pinto licked Cade's hand, receiving a quick pat on the
head in return. "Looks like you gave him a good workout. He needs some exercise."

"He's pretty fast for someone his age." Davey gave a
low whistle, which brought the dog back to his side.
"Can we come back tomorrow? I mean to play. There's
more space here than at Luna's. I mean if we're still
around?" Warily, his eyes sought my permission.

"Sure. Anytime you want to. But you might be coming back next week anyway. Your mom will talk to you about that."

Davey's grin said he was glad we'd be staying here for at least a week, and he nodded at me with grateful eyes. Cade placed our coffee cups in the sink and left to join Luna in the room down the hall. Davey sat down in the seat he'd left.

"So we can stay?"

"For a while. A couple of weeks, maybe."

"What about—?" He didn't need to finish.

"We'll figure something out." It felt good to say that, telling him that we wouldn't run, at least not right away. But his quick, doubtful glance told me otherwise, and I nodded, acknowledging that we couldn't talk about it here, not in front of anybody. I told him then what Cade and I had talked about, explaining that he had gotten too far behind at school and needed to catch up. He scrunched his lips, letting me know whom he wanted to blame for that, even though I knew he really didn't blame me, except on bad days when he needed someone to be mad at.

"So what's he going to teach me?"

"Anything you want to learn. Stuff that will help you next time we need to—"

"But you just said we wouldn't have to leave again!" Anger sparked in his eyes. "You just said it!"

"I know what I said, and I didn't say that, not exactly."

"Almost exactly. So where did Luna go?" He was defiant now but hid it. Like Pinto, Luna was quickly becoming an ally. I'd heard the two of them laughing together when I came downstairs for breakfast. I had no idea what they were talking about, but it had been good to hear his laughter. He was as at ease with Luna as he was with her dog, and I was reminded again how narrow our lives were, how thin and devoid of fun. Except for school, I was his only company.

When Anna was alive, she'd been there for him, too, in ways I never could. She'd understood him because of the bond—the shifting "gift"—they shared. He would tilt his head sometimes, in the weeks after she died, listening for a sound sung or whispered at a timbre I couldn't hear. It scared me at first, that some unspoken secret seemed to be calling him, a thing that shut me out. I'd wondered how deep those family ties went, how deeply he was bound to Anna, even after death.

Recently, the listening had grown less. Only every now and then would I catch him picking up his head, waiting for the voice of someone gone. But then he'd drop it when he saw me looking, unwilling to let me between them. Maybe Luna could become like Anna, with her own strange song to sing my lonely son, yet safer. Luna was bound to me by blood, so I'd be part of that song; I would hear it, too.

"So what were you and Luna laughing about in the kitchen this morning?" I asked, knowing he wouldn't tell me. Secrets were too big a part of our lives.

"Between me and Luna. So where did she go?"

"Down the hall," I said, letting him have his space. "But knock if the door is closed."

"Why would the door be closed?" With Pinto at his

heels, he headed down the hall, and I heard him rapping hard, then entering when nobody answered.

"Don't come in here!" Luna yelled, too late.

He had run inside, the dog prancing ahead of him, and then I heard him stop and scream, the sound as sharp and piercing as it always was when he was afraid. I ran down the hall and into the room, snatching him toward me.

It was Pinto who knew he was shifting. His growl told me that, and his snarl, those little teeth sharp and white as he backed away from Davey almost into the wall. I pulled Davey close to me, as big as he was, trying to hide him from the dog, from anything that could hurt him.

"Pinto!" Luna screamed. Whimpering but obedient, the dog slunk toward her, head down, but his eyes, so wide and friendly before, glared angrily and fiercely at Davey now. Davey was afraid, too. But it wasn't Pinto that scared him. He had seen or sensed something in the room, and I felt his body changing against my own: his limbs shrinking ever so slightly, fist balling, mouth puckering against my breast like that of some beast he knew he would become.

"Don't, Davey." I bent and whispered in his ear. "Don't. Don't. Breathe like you tell me to do when I'm scared. Breathe to stop it from happening. Nothing is here. I will keep you safe."

He couldn't speak. His voice was lost somewhere deep inside him.

Pinto growled from across the room, snapping, snarling at the air.

"Stop it!" Luna ordered the dog as she whacked him across his snout, then grabbed his collar, holding him tight.

I pushed Davey into the hall as far away from the door as I could, then stepped into the room lit by the morning sun pouring in through the curtain-less windows. A wedding picture sat on the desk. Cade and a pretty woman with a wide, bright smile. Stacks of paper and unopened folders piled around them, and on a small table in a far corner, dried daisies bunched in a white china vase.

"Go sit on the couch and wait for me, now!" I whispered to Davey.

"No! Mom, I'm scared." He had found his voice, but it had changed. It was deeper, with a hoarseness to it.

"I'll be right there. Go," I said, and he left, his body shaking as he tried to control what had begun to happen. Pinto growled again, barking at Davey as he left. Davey looked back at him, and the sadness in his eyes pulled deep into my heart.

"Stop it, you foolish little beast!" Luna snapped, and Pinto, suddenly cowed, kneeled at her feet.

"What the hell is going on?" Cade stepped forward, his eyes wide as he confronted first me, then Luna. "What's wrong with Davey? How come he ran like that?"

I said nothing. An object on the desk had caught my attention, a piece of a claw that lay a few inches from the wedding photograph, bone gray and as grotesque as the one I'd seen at Anna's house all those years ago; the one wrapped in white cotton kept inside a lead box. They do that sometimes, Anna had told me. Leave bits of themselves behind to warn those who need to be warned, scare them before they tell their secrets. It was a token; its spirit still within. You can tell if you feel it, she said as she'd grabbed my hand, making me touch the horrible thing. I was back into that memory now, of her rough fingers grasping mine, of the sharp edge of the thing, which looked like a fingernail, when it pricked my finger, drew my blood. Never forget this, she told me. This is what you must protect him from.

I looked at Cade and fear shot through me. How was he tied to the creature? Had I nearly given him my child? "What are you?" I said to him, barely able to speak.

"What do you mean, what *am* I? Luna?" His gaze, unfaltering and angry, had shot to Luna for an answer.

Luna answered, quietly but firmly. "You two are as bad as this damn dog. Both of you calm down," she said. "Cade is fine. He's just what he looks like. Children and animals have a sixth sense that picks up things we don't. Something sad or evil happened here, and they know it."

"What happened here?" I was the one who needed answers now.

"And what do you mean asking what I am, what are you talking about?" His voice rose as he confronted me; annoyance verging on anger was in his eyes.

"Davey is waiting in the living room, and he's scared." I was afraid of him now, unwilling to answer or even look at him.

"Why is he so scared?" Cade turned to Luna. "How could he possibly know—?"

"Rooms have memories, like people do, that linger

even when what happened is over. And Pinto? Spooked by his new buddy's fear."

A good liar, I thought. Good enough for him, but not for me. The thing on the desk told me that. My first instinct was right—take my kid and run like I always did. Cade followed me as I started to leave and grabbed my shoulder. It was a strange touch, gentle but insistent, an answer to a question that wasn't asked. I faced him, gazed into his eyes, not sure what I would find, and saw kindness and curiosity—no evil at all.

"This used to be my wife's office," he said. "I found her here after she died. It's been closed a long time. I haven't been able to come in here much. Maybe there was something about it . . . I don't know. There's a lot of grief still here. Maybe that's still there. Luna's the expert on weird stuff like that, kids and animals sensing sorrow. Maybe there's something to it."

"Mom, are you okay?" Davey called me from the living room. Fear was in his voice because he was as scared for me as I had been for him. The three of us left the room, Luna slamming the door behind her.

"You okay, man?" Cade sat down beside Davey on the coach.

"I'm good." Davey hid his fear, manning up, the way boys do. His senses about what stalked us were stronger than mine, and he sensed no danger from Cade. His normalcy calmed me down.

Luna, holding Pinto tightly, brought him toward the couch, but it was Davey who pulled away, fear plain on his face. "He's a silly old dog, sometimes," Luna explained. "He gets scared just like you do. Here, come close."

"Luna, I—"

"He's fine now," Luna said. "Let him sniff your hand, and he'll see that you're okay." Davey searched my face for an answer.

"*Are* you okay?" I asked, and he nodded.

"Here," Luna let go of Pinto's collar. He hesitated, then ran toward Davey, and when Davey dropped his hand, he gave it an enthusiastic lick.

"Watch him, though," Luna warned. "He doesn't have good sense. You know what I'm talking about."

"Okay." He wasn't sure if he could trust the dog again, and neither was I, but for now things were okay, and the now was all we had some days.

❧

Later that night, after dinner, Davey and I settled down in our room.

"It's still looking for us, isn't it?" he said. He lay in the trundle bed that pulled out, and I sat on the edge of mine, pretending to read a magazine and waiting for him to go to sleep. I didn't need to answer. He was smart, like I'd told Cade; he knew the deal. There was enough of Anna still in him to know the truth. "It's going to kill me, isn't it?"

I found my voice, put some strength into it. "No. I think we've lost it, and if it finds us, I'm not going to let it."

"But it won't be up to you," he said quietly and with a certainty that alarmed me. "Are we going to run again?"

"How you feeling?" I wasn't ready to answer that yet.

"Pinto knows, about me." He turned over in his bed, his voice deep like it gets when he's weighed down by sadness.

"Yeah, I guess he does."

"But he still played with me—later on, I mean."

"That was a good thing."

"So Luna knows, too?"

"Some of it."

"How about Cade?"

"No, and don't tell him anything either, understand?"

As soon as he fell asleep, I checked my phone for Mack's message. Someone had called him, looking for me, and he wanted to know if he should tell them where I was. I erased the message, not answering back. He thought I was on my way to Baltimore, and as long as I went nowhere near that restaurant, nowhere near that part of town, that was all he had to know. It was up to me to keep our secret.

5

cade

The howl, so low and deep in the animal's throat, woke Cade up and sent a shiver down his back. Poor thing must be hurt, he thought. It was three in the morning, but when he looked out the bedroom window, there was nothing to be seen, yet he couldn't get rid of the sound; it echoed in his mind. Could it be Pinto? he wondered. But the snarl at the end of it told him it was a larger animal, a fiercer one, with teeth. Why had that notion occurred to him at all? Why would a bark make him think about teeth, fangs, like a wolf might have?

It was back an hour later, a whimper this time, a baleful cry that twitched his heart because it made him think of how Dennie always threatened to take in some stray, tame it, make it part of their family, and he cried, swallowing sobs because he realized that he was and always had been the stray in Dennie's life; she'd taken him in, opened her heart, then broken his with her death.

So when the growl came back at first light, just as dawn was breaking, he lay still and listened to it, took it in, opening himself up to it like he knew she would have done. Maybe he'd put out some food in the morning, lure it close enough to pet, maybe even tame it. Davey might like that, a dog that was really a dog not a toy poodle like Pinto, bless his heart, with the occasional pink bow fixed on top of his head. The kid needed a rough-and-tumble dog, the kind that could catch a hard-thrown ball, like Blaze used to, the copper Lab his neighbor had had when Cade was a kid. Davey deserved a dog like that, and maybe someday if his mama could make up her mind about coming or going, maybe he'd have it. Here it was nearly July fourth and as far as he could tell, Raine hadn't decided one way or the other. Not a good thing to hang on a kid—not knowing where he'd be the next year or the one following—especially a kid as sharp as Davey. But it wasn't his place to comment.

They met three times a week, he and Davey—Tuesdays, Thursdays, Saturdays—which surprised Cade because sitting around with a tutor was the last thing most boys would want to do on a Saturday afternoon, not with balls to toss and races to run and general mischief to plan. Raine suggested four times a week, more tutoring than any boy should endure, as far as he was concerned, so they compromised on three. He could tell Davey looked forward to their sessions, and truth be told, so did he. Cade missed the routine of school, the spirited horseplay and giggles of the kids he taught. The house was too damn quiet, too filled with sorrow for him to enjoy his solitude. And Davey wasn't a typical child. He was mature in surprising ways and even though he was a kid, good company.

Most of Cade's friends were married and had quietly deserted him after Dennie's death, and his single friends—obsessed with fast women and faster sports—had little to offer in support or real friendship. Luna was his best friend these days, and he suspected even she grew weary of the burden of his grief.

Davey usually showed up a half an hour ahead of time, eager to start his lessons early. After working at the kitchen table, they'd sit around the living room to watch a ball game, play video games (definitely not on the list of things teachers were supposed to encourage), and more recently, a game or two of chess. The boy was a quick study, picking up various moves and openings faster than any kid he'd ever seen. He, himself, loved the game. His father had taught him to play, one of the few things they'd done together when his old man wasn't drunk—and sometimes even when he was. He'd been thinking about his father more than usual these days; Davey's presence, even for this brief time, had brought his father back in ways that surprised him. He'd even dreamed about him recently, a pleasant one, not like so many of the others. They'd been sitting on a porch (he had no idea where that came from; they'd never lived in a house), playing chess, talking about nothing, and he felt a grinning kind of happiness, the kind he'd never known as a kid.

His father was the reason he had volunteered to become an advisor for the chess club at school, and when he taught Davey strategies and moves, he found himself using some of the same words and examples his father had with him. It was clear the boy had talent, just as he had. His father used to say he'd be the first black Grandmaster. He hadn't gone that far, but Cade held his own in tournaments, the same way this kid would if he put his mind to it.

The queen, the most important piece on the board, was the predictable favorite of most kids—his father liked bishops. Davey preferred knights and pawns, the weakest pieces.

"So how come you like those guys?" Cade, puzzled by his choice, had asked.

"Because a knight can move in weird, secretive ways, and a pawn—well that guy can be a queen, and then you got two."

"It takes a lot of luck for a pawn to make it to the eighth rank," he'd cautioned. "But you're right about one thing: Even a weak piece can have more power than his enemy realizes, if the player plays the piece well, uses his head more than his heart.

"A good player lures him in, plays him for a fool. Lets him have your bishop so you can get his queen. You've got to see at least four moves in the future, four moves down the board, so you can win."

"Pawns should get more props than they do," Davey said as he pushed his black pawn into position to challenge Cade's white bishop, which made Cade grin. "It can kick your ass before you know you been kicked." Amused, Cade chuckled at the boy's choice of words; he was sure Davey didn't use them around his mother.

Like most boys his age, Davey spewed curse words as much as he could after testing Cade's response, and he'd recognized that for what it was—the stuff kids usually did around their friends. But as far as he could tell, the boy didn't have any—no kids came to visit, no video parlor dates, nothing. Davey and Raine rarely left Luna's house, and when they did, it was always in the early morning, and that puzzled and worried him. Kids needed to be around other kids, to curse, bounce ideas, brew up trouble, and this kid was lonely and hungry for company and that made him vulnerable.

Last Saturday, he'd asked Davey if he would like to join a study group. There were several kids from last year's class whose parents had begged him to tutor, and at the time, the thought of prolonging the school year and dealing with unruly preteens was more than he could handle, but now it didn't seem such a bad idea. Davey was smart enough to hold his own with boys his own age; it would do them all some good. He'd ask Davey first—kids, particularly lonely ones like him, could be possessive, and he didn't want to put a strain on their relationship. When their session was over, they'd started a game of chess. Davey had just captured one of his rooks, taking him by surprise.

"So what do you think about studying with a few other kids?" he'd asked, closely watching his reaction.

Davey stiffened and shook his head, staring down at the board. "My mom wants me to do that?"

"No, it's my idea."

"Naw, that would be weird," he'd said to the board, chin propped in his hand as he concentrated. "And they'd probably think I was weird."

"Weird? How come they'd think that?"

"Because I am." An amused glint sparkled in Davey's eyes behind his new glasses. He'd recently replaced his Harry Potter specs with "cooler" glasses.

"Not any weirder than anybody else," Cade had said, painful memories from his own childhood shooting through him. His shame about his father had made him too shy to reach out. He was also small for his age, and easy to bully. "Weird" would have been one of the nicer things kids called him. "Everybody is weird sometimes."

"Not weird like me."

"So what makes you weirder than anybody else?"

Davey shrugged, and Cade continued. "It's not because you're biracial, is it? Everybody has a little bit of everybody else in them. Like the president. Look at him! Be proud of every part of you." Cade wondered if the boy knew much about his Navajo heritage and was thinking that might be a good thing for them to focus on in their studies. "My wife was into Navajo history and mythology. That was what she was studying."

"For real?"

"Yeah."

"But she died, right?"

"Yeah. She did." Davey's question had surprised and puzzled him.

"Check!" Davey said, skirting his bishop to challenge Cade's king and change the subject. When they first began to play, he'd let Davey win nearly every game. Not anymore.

"Not quite!" Cade defended his king with his queen, and Davey chuckled with an impish grin. "Good move, though."

They'd played in silence for a while, Cade thinking about Dennie and wishing he hadn't brought her up. He glanced at Davey, tried another question.

"So do your *friends* think you're weird, too, or just the plain, run-of-the-mill kids?"

Davey took a sip from the glass of apple juice sitting on the table beside the board. It was a tiny sip, and Cade smiled to himself. He'd never seen a kid who could make a glass of juice last so long.

"Plain, run-of-the-mill kids."

"But not your good friends, right?"

"Nope, not them. But, like, I only had, like, two *good* friends here. Plus, I never showed them my weird side."

"Have I ever seen it?"

Davey shrugged. "If you saw it, you'd know it."

Cade waited a minute or two, and then asked, "How would I know I was seeing it?"

"You just would."

"Like, what school were you at, anyway?"

"Across town," Davey said too quickly.

"Where across town?"

It had been a cheap attempt to find out more than was offered, and Davey wasn't fooled; he shrugged again. Cade knew enough about kids to leave it alone, but still wondered about a boy so full of secrets and if he'd ever trust him enough to share what was bothering him. And Raine, too. Something was always eating at her, seemed like she was always just a beat away from turning tail and running. He'd noticed that when she'd linger for a quick chat about Davey's progress after their sessions.

He'd never inquired about her future plans, and she

didn't offer them. Once, he'd casually asked what school Davey was registered to attend in the fall, and she told him she hadn't yet decided. If it's around here, I'd be glad to reach out to his teachers, he'd said, and she cut him off, smiling shyly, studying her cup of tea as assiduously as Davey studied the chessboard, a glass of apple juice, or his hands, when he had no other prop. She'd let him know when she decided, she said, and that had been that. He knew she wouldn't. He feared Davey and Raine would probably leave his life as quickly and unexpectedly as they'd entered it.

Truth be told, he'd begun to look forward to tea with Raine as much as he did his time with her son. He admired her interest in her son's progress, so different from many of the parents whose children he taught during the year. She hungered for every detail: what he liked and didn't, if he paid attention, if he was on the same level as other kids, and he was happy to assure her that he was at or above level and reading on a high school level. She grinned when he said that, a lopsided happy grin that delighted him. Davey has always been a reader, she said, just like his father was; she'd let that slip, then stopped, unwilling to reveal anything else.

That made Cade wonder about this father whom Davey never mentioned and Raine avoided talking about. What had happened to him? How had he died? Several days later, he'd approached Luna. Their backyards were separated by bushes, now summer-green and free of lilacs. He spotted her watering herbs and flowers in her backyard and called out to her.

"So why don't you just straight-out ask her about

him?" she'd said through the hedges as she trimmed the tops off an odd-smelling plant with a name he couldn't pronounce. She was dressed in a pink gingham sundress that looked like it came from the 1950s, something he'd never seen her in before. It was a sunny afternoon, surprisingly hot for the end of June, one of those rare occasions when Davey and Raine had gone out—to the mall, Luna told him, because Davey had outgrown his clothes and needed things for the summer.

"They both seem uncomfortable talking about him."

"What exactly did you ask them?" He could barely see her face through the bushes, and he was tempted to go into her yard but sensed closer proximity would do no good.

"Well, nothing, exactly. They just made it clear they didn't want to talk about him."

"People tell you as much as they want you to know and leave out the rest. If and when she wants you to know more, she'll tell you."

"So *you* know, then?"

"You're a big hit around here, I'll tell you that. Davey was bragging last night at dinner that he beats the hell out of you every time you play chess," she'd said, gracelessly changing the subject.

"Well, not every time."

"Thanks for taking them in." Luna had come closer and peered at him through a break in the bushes. Her eyes seemed tired, sad. "Didn't I tell you that more people needed you than you thought? You need them, too, don't you?"

"Well, I—"

"I'm sick of seeing you sit around that house by yourself. Dennie wouldn't want that."

"No, she wouldn't." The mere mention of his wife's name had darkened his mood.

"I'm usually right about stuff like that. Why don't you take Raine out for some coffee somewhere or a drink? Away from that house and this one. Davey can stay with me. It will do you all good."

"Raine mentioned that people in her family have a gift, she called it, knowing, sensing things that most people don't, but she said she didn't have it," he said, not responding to Luna's suggestion.

"Really?" Luna chuckled. "The women in my family do have gifts, and if Raine had it, she'd know it . . . and so would you."

If you saw it, you'd know it.

"So you obviously have it, that gift Raine was talking about?"

"You don't know the half of it," Luna muttered, and went back into her house.

❧

Cade remembered Luna's words now, as he waited for Davey to ring the bell. Maybe he didn't need to know the half of it. He'd decided to barbecue some ribs on the Fourth, something he and Dennie used to do even though most of the time, she called herself a vegetarian. But he could always tempt her with a chicken leg. He smiled when he thought of that, how he loved to tease her. He wondered if Raine was a vegetarian, too. He knew

Luna wasn't. Despite her love of herbal teas and vegetarian soups, he'd seen her gobble down ribs with the best of them. He glanced at the clock. Davey was late today. He was picking up the phone to call when the doorbell rang.

Something was different about the boy today; a shadow hung around his eyes and made Cade wonder if he'd gotten enough sleep or was coming down with something.

"So how you doing?" he asked, trying to sound casual as they sat down at the kitchen table. "Did I give you too much homework?"

"No, it was okay." Davey wouldn't look at him.

"Okay, let's get started. Let me see what you got." Cade took the papers the boy had stuffed into a folder and quickly evaluated them. The writing was sloppy, common for boys his age, but the report on Severus Snape, from the Harry Potter series, was insightful and clever. His choice of Snape, the complex half-blood wizard, was revealing, too, confirming his suspicion that there were layers to Davey's life he kept deep inside.

That, too, reminded him of himself when he was a kid and his shame about his old man's drunkenness haunted everything he did, and yet at the same time he'd loved and worshipped his father as only a boy can, despite his failings. That had haunted him, too. When he was Davey's age, he'd told more than one of his few friends that his father was dead, killed in the war, never saying which one. Kids love their parent no matter how bad they are, Dennie, the explainer of all contradictions, would tell him, but Dennie, blessed with charming, loving parents, had no sense of what an ugly childhood could be like. Raine said that Davey's father had died before he was born; maybe her love for Davey's father was as colored by shame as his for his father had been.

Cade glanced up as Davey yawned, head dropping down to his chest.

"Hey, man, wake up! Didn't you get enough sleep last night? That crazy dog howling like a fool must have kept you up, too." His scolding was playful, but the terror on Davey's face at his words startled him. "Hey, come on, you're too old to be scared of an old whiny dog."

"You heard it, too?" Davey's eyes pleaded, searching for an answer.

"Sure I heard it. Probably woke up half the neighborhood."

"Wasn't just a dog." Davey's voice was dull, frightened.

"Yeah it was, Davey. You been watching too much Chiller TV."

"Don't tell Mom, okay? Please don't tell Mom!"

"About the TV? Cause you were scared? Listen, Davey, stuff scares people all the time. Grown men, like me, get scared by stuff."

That was for damn sure. That was for goddamn sure.

"No, about the dog. Don't tell her about the dog!" There was a tremor in the boy's voice, something he'd never heard before.

"Why?"

"Just don't."

"Okay, so I guess it didn't wake her up?"

"Just me." The darkness that had shadowed Davey's eyes spread to his face.

"And me," Cade added with a slow smile. "Don't worry, Davey, your secret is safe with me."

They worked awhile longer, until it was clear that Davey was too tired to keep his eyes open. When he went to the bathroom down the hall, Cade heard him pause before the closed door—the one to Dennie's office—hesitating as if listening for something inside, until his quick, hurried footsteps echoed down the hallway. The boy's eyes were red when he returned, as if he'd been crying.

"Let's call it a day," Cade said, and Davey nodded. Without answering, he gathered up books and papers and headed out the door. There would be no chess or even apple juice today. "See you tomorrow?" Cade yelled before the door closed, but it was too late; Davey was across the front lawn to Luna's house, head bowed low as if studying the ground on which he walked.

Please don't tell Mom.

Later that night when Cade lay in bed, he could still hear the terror in Davey's voice, and he listened for the howl of the dog that had put such fear into the boy's eyes.

6

raine

"It found us," Davey said.

I never wanted to hear those words, and they pierced my heart like a stab.

I was sitting on the rusty swing in Luna's backyard, sketching the irises blooming in the middle of Luna's small garden. Once upon a time in the beginning of my crazy life, I was going to be an artist, that was what I called myself the day I met Elan. What do you do? he'd asked, and I, so sure of everything in life, said, I draw things. I'm an artist. And that was how he always thought of me. Drawing still brought peace some days, taking down what I've seen, putting it on paper. So I kept my eyes on the flowers and the branches that tipped across the fence into the yard next door—Cade's backyard.

"How did it go at Cade's?" I asked, ignoring what he'd said.

"Mom, are you listening? Did you hear what I told you? I heard it last night. It was outside the window. I heard it growling, and it's coming for me, for us, I know it is." He squeezed next to me, his voice and eyes angry and frightened, and then he began to cry. It had been years since Davey let me see him cry, but he did now, breaking into sobs that shook his body. I put down my sketch pad, grabbed him tightly so nothing would happen, so he wouldn't begin to shift.

"Mom, we tried to run away, and it *still* found us."

"Maybe it was just a dog," I said. "Just some foolish old dog howling at the moon." But I knew better than that; we both did.

"That's what Cade said. But it wasn't."

"Cade heard it, too?" I stiffened.

"Yeah. So I know it's real."

I had begun to feel safe here with Luna and her occasional sprinklings of white ash around her house and yard, her burning of incense and rubbing of oil. I didn't understand what she did or why she did it, but I felt it protected us, and when she'd uttered those words about "figuring something out" all those weeks ago, I tried to believe her. Just sitting here and swinging back and forth in her creaky old swing made me feel as if Davey and I *could* lead a normal life. He felt that way, too. Luna's backyard was one of the places we both loved. I wasn't ready to risk Davey's life, though. Anna's words about not trusting anybody, the warning to keep running, were etched too deep inside me.

And I had other reasons to be wary. I'd glimpsed a woman who looked like Anna walking past Cade's house, but she vanished before I got a good look. As I was driving down the street two weeks ago, I'd stopped for a light and happened to look in the car beside me and saw her again, hair as long and straight as iron, like Anna's had been, and when she turned to look at me, her eyes had been as hard and round but with no glimmer of love like Anna's had had. She raised her hand as if waving or beckoning, and a chill went through me. Could it be the cousin I'd met at Anna's funeral, begging me to stay? Had she found me? Something told me to flee, and I did, driving wildly, turning one corner and then the next until I dared to look in the rear window again. I must have imagined the whole thing, I told myself. Anna was dead; her family— the "filthy pack," as she once called them—lived far away. I had nothing to fear from them.

The last time was more sense than sighting. There had been a smell that day, lingering in the air. Not unpleasant, a familiar one I couldn't place. A hint of pine trees and wildflower honey touched with the herbs with which Anna used to cook. Davey had been with me that day, walking from Luna's car toward the house, and he stopped short, sensing it, too. He lifted his head as if sniffing the air, a puzzled expression on his face. He leaned his head forward, as he so often did with Anna, listening to something I couldn't hear, but when he saw me watching, he straightened up, all expression gone, and said nothing.

But I was sure I was imagining those things. I couldn't let myself believe anything else. When it had come before, it made its presence known, it wasn't subtle or secretive.

Davey moved close now like he used to do when he was young and believed I was his defending, avenging angel—even though Anna was the real protector. I knew it and so had he as he grew older. But Anna was gone.

"What did Cade say about it?"

"Just asked me if it kept me up, too, howling like it did, and I said it had."

I pulled away, looking him in the eye because I needed the truth. "You didn't tell him anything about us, did you?"

"No."

"You know that even if you like somebody, you can't—"

"Mom, I didn't tell him!"

I eased back from his anger. "You know—"

"Mom, you've told me that all my stupid life!"

We sat apart now, not touching, and filling me with sadness. I wondered again, as I always did when this separateness sometimes came between us, what kind of life Davey could lead.

As if he could read my thoughts, he sighed heavily, like an old man does. "I think it got Cade's wife," he said.

"Maybe not."

"I know it did, Mom. It got his wife like it got my dad."

I'd never told him how Elan had died—how could I? Had Anna said something in her determination to protect him, to make him seek vengeance someday?

"It was there in the room that day, you know when Pinto got scared. She died in that room that scared me."

I went back to drawing the irises in the garden, forcing steadiness back into my hand and voice. "I think she was sick, that was how she died. Did Cade tell you that something killed her?"

His smile came slowly, as if he was relieved, glad I was telling him something he wanted to believe. I rattled on like I believed it, too. "People get sick sometimes and die for no reason. Like your dad did. Just because you heard a dog growl at night doesn't mean it found us. And anyway, we're nowhere near that church where you saw it. And even where I used to work. Nobody knows where we are. We're way across town, not anywhere near it."

"But what about the room? His wife died in that room, didn't she?"

"What makes you say that?"

"Remember when I went in there, how I got scared, how . . . how . . . you know what happened! Don't you remember?"

I took my time answering him because there would be no calling my words back once they were spoken. Davey's mind was like a trap; once something was said, he kept it inside him forever. Like Anna, who never forgot a slight or favor or threat.

It hadn't been that long ago, but I could only remember snatches of that day and what I'd seen in the room. The wedding picture—the sweet-faced bride and happy Cade, the books and papers on the desk. I hadn't talked to Luna about any of it—like the bone-gray thing that looked so much like the one at Anna's house, the bit of itself that had been left behind. I'd told myself I was mistaken. Davey hadn't seen it; if he had, he would have mentioned it. His concern had been Pinto turning on him like he had. He hadn't heard Luna's words about kids and animals sensing evil things. I'd had doubts about Cade that day, and for an instant I remembered the queasy feeling I'd gotten in my stomach when I saw the thing, wondered how Cade was tied to it, if I was mistaken and he was linked to the danger that threatened us.

I looked my son squarely in the eye. "No, I don't know exactly what happened that day, why don't you tell me?"

"I was scared."

"I remember that. Why were you scared?"

He looked perplexed. "I don't remember. I started shifting then, and I don't remember stuff when I shift. It takes over my mind."

"I think it was because of Pinto's foolishness, remember? Because of the way he turned on you."

Puzzled, Davey nodded after a moment. "But I felt something else, too, Mom. I knew it had been there. I know it's here now."

"But have you seen it, actually seen it?"

"No," he said in a voice I could barely hear. I shrugged, forced a smile. "Every time you hear a dog bark, you don't want to get scared, do you? You're too old for that, right?"

"Then we don't have to leave?"

His fear of leaving was right up there with his fear of it. "Let's just wait and see."

His eyes grew doubtful again. "How long?"

"Let's just wait and see," I said, forcing another carefree shrug. Leaving it alone, I went back to my drawing. After a while, Davey went inside, and I heard him talking to Luna, and when they both began to laugh, I took one of Davey's breaths, telling myself we would be okay after all, that growling dogs come and go. But I knew I needed to find out exactly what had happened to Cade's wife.

So later that night, I joined Luna in the living room

for her evening cordial, as she liked to call the drink she had before she went to her room to watch TV and read. It was usually a glass of malbec or cabernet (only one, she'd always say, to be drunk after seven o'clock) sipped peacefully and silently as she sat on the couch, staring into space. Sometimes it was a cup of chamomile tea— always in a fancy china teacup streaked with silver and roses with its matching saucer—and every now and then, when she'd had a hard day at the small accounting firm where she worked part-time, it was a Bloody Mary lavishly flavored with Worcestershire sauce and a thin slice of lime. It was tea tonight, which always put her in a meditative mood.

Luna smiled when I came into the room. Come and sit with me she said, and I told her I would and that I needed to talk to her for a minute or two. I rarely joined her at night. When Davey was in bed, I usually settled down on my bed to read magazines or the paperback mysteries Luna kept in abundance. I tried to give her as much space as I could. She'd taken us in with no request for money and no clear sense of when we planned to leave. Yes, we were family, those folks who couldn't be turned down when they showed up at the door, but I knew we must be an inconvenience even though she never said it. Davey, in a growth spurt, was eating everything he could get his hands on, and Luna made sure he was well fed. I'd asked her more than once to let me help out with the money, but she refused. You got other things to think of, she'd said, and she was right, I did.

When Anna died, her cousin Doba begged me to stay with her in Anna's house, but I had too many memories and needed to leave. The look in her eyes when she stared at Davey told me she'd try to control us the same way Anna had, for the good and the bad. If I was ever going to be on my own, I'd have to go now. She'd put the money Anna left us in the bank, and told me when I needed it, all I had to do was let her and the bank know. My plans were to let it sit there and grow until Davey needed it for school, and in all the years I'd been running, I'd only asked that cash be wired a couple of times—last time being six months ago, around Christmas. Maybe it was time to do it again.

When I asked Luna about it now, she still wouldn't hear of it. "What did I tell you before?" she said, and I thanked her again, although I wasn't surprised. I poured myself a cup of tea before I asked her my next question, the one I really needed her to answer.

"How did Cade's wife die?" I said after a few long sips.

Surprised, Luna's eyes fastened on me like mine had been on Davey earlier; then her gaze dropped down to her cup. "Why don't you ask him?"

"Because I'm asking you." I took a sip of tea and Luna did the same, but her hand shook when she placed it in her saucer.

"Nerves, that's all," she said, but I knew better. She brought the cup back up to her lips, hand as steady as ever, proving steadiness to herself as well as to me.

"You don't want to talk about it, do you?"

"I'll tell you the same thing I told him last week. You got your story, he got his. Best thing for you both to do is to talk to each other if you want to know each other's business. It's not mine to tell."

"He wanted to know something about *me*?" Anxiety swept through me as it always did, and I didn't bother to hide the suspicious tone. "You didn't tell him anything, did you? About Davey? About—"

"Of course not!"

"What did he want to know, exactly?"

"Ask him."

I paused to put some honey into my tea. "That day when we were in the room, the room where Davey got scared, you said something sad or evil could linger in a place. Was she fatally ill? His wife?"

It took Luna a while to answer that, and when she did it was with a sigh that came out slow and heavy. "No, only if you believe that curiosity can kill a cat."

"Curiosity?"

"That's what I said."

I waited before I asked her more. "Cade said you and she were friends."

"Friends then, still are," Luna added with a half smile meant to leave me wondering; I knew better than to ask. Luna was younger than Anna by more than twenty years but had the same reserved, secretive ways, the ones that hinted you had to be more grown than you were to share her thoughts. I'd learned not to resent it with Anna, and I didn't now with Luna. You took her as she was or not at all. So I sipped the rest of my tea in silence, patiently waiting for her to say whatever she was going to add.

"She was a kind lady with a heart and mind bigger than it should have been. Always one to take in lonely beings, like middle-aged women new to a closed neighborhood, and anything else that needed a home."

"She was a teacher like Cade?"

"No, she was in school herself. A cultural anthropologist, interested in Native American myths, old stories, stuff that makes no sense in the world we live in. We had a lot in common." She smiled her half smile as if remembering something pleasant.

"Davey thinks what killed his father killed her, too," I said, throwing it out fast, studying Luna closely for a reaction.

Luna's eyes changed, looked away and then into mine, and then she gave a weak smile. "Is that what Davey said? Your boy has more of our people in him than you think," she said finally. "All I really know about Dennie's death is what I saw the night I went there. It wasn't illness that killed her."

"Is Davey right?" A chill went through me.

"I don't know, but he might be."

"It's time for us to leave," I said more to myself than to her. "We can't stay here anymore. If it killed his wife, it's closer than it should be."

"Dennie died a year ago."

"But somehow these things must be tied. Dennie's wife, us living next door. Something is drawing it to us."

"Talk to Cade before you drag that boy all over kingdom come again," Luna said gently. "Think about what you're doing. He's going to need his strength to fight it, and he's got to find it here. From you. Everybody else is dead. I sure can't teach him. He'll learn from you, Raine, to stand up like he has to. You're the only hope he has, Raine, and maybe Cade, if you give him time to get involved in the child's life."

I was stunned by her words, but there was tenderness in her eyes, too, when they met mine. "He might know more than he thinks about his wife's death, something that will help you, and you may have less time than you think."

"Why do you say that? About the time?"

"It's the way things work, in patterns. Dennie died in April a year ago. Full moon the night of her death, I remember that," she said, not fully answering my questions, then continued. "You two—you and Cade—are tied in some essential way, I know that. Nothing happens in life without a reason, and you've found each other for reasons that neither of you know. But both of you need the courage to find out what it is, decide for yourselves. I can't do it. That much I do know. Call him. He's still up. I know that, too."

Without another word, she picked up our cups and went into the kitchen and I heard the clang of the china cups in the sink. It was hard to tell whether she was annoyed with me, Cade, or the world in general. It was like that sometimes with Luna.

But I did call Cade and we agreed to meet for coffee at the Starbucks down the street the next day.

Davey had moved into his own room earlier in the summer, and Luna had insisted that he fix it up any way he wanted to. He'd always had a room of his own. I slept on a pullout couch in the living room and let him have the bedroom in our apartments, but we'd never been able to paint or hang things on the wall, which he did here with abandon. The walls were navy blue, nearly black at night, with red trim on the windows and sheets and blankets to match. Posters of his favorite heroes—Harry Potter, the Olympians, had lately been replaced with those of heavy metal bands I'd never heard of—hung on the walls. His books were neatly stacked on a bookshelf in the corner, and Luna's old computer was on his desk. Pinto had abandoned Luna's room for his, and slept most nights on a pillow next to the closet.

I entered quietly, careful not to wake Davey. He was tired and had gone to bed early. I bent down to kiss him on his cheek. He stirred, opening one eye, then closing it. "You'll be okay," I whispered in his ear, not sure why I said it.

I tried hard to believe it myself.

7

raine

Funny how summer days repeat themselves—the scent of cotton candy lingering somewhere in the air, a light breeze occasionally fanning just the side of your left cheek. This one brought back the day I'd met Elan all those years ago, the anticipation of hot days, cold drinks, and good things to come. I hadn't allowed myself to enjoy a summer's day since he died, but I recalled it now—the lightness and joy I felt that day—when Cade and I settled at one of the Starbucks' outside tables. The place was close enough to walk if you were in a walking mood, and we'd been in walking moods. Walking gave me a chance to consider what I'd say to him when we got there—about his wife, about how she died. I was curious about her, Dennie, the pretty girl in that wedding photograph, and that had made me remember me and Elan on our wedding day, the careless joy I'd felt that I would never feel again.

When I sat across from him, coffee in a paper cup, almond biscotti on a plate in front of us, I felt more like a woman on a date than an interrogator. It was three, too late for lunch and too early for dinner, not quite this or the other, and the day and time made me feel happy, almost carefree, and that surprised me. I had to remind myself that this was a meeting, nothing more, though neither of us had said what it was about.

I hadn't thought of it as a date but ended up dressing for one. My white blouse had only been worn once, and my tan linen pants—cool and well tailored—were stylishly snug yet meant to ward off July's heat. A silver chain Davey gave me for my birthday (money lent by Mack) was a good match for the silver earrings that had once belonged to Anna. They were fancy ones, intertwined with gold twirled decoratively around a turquoise the size of a marble. There was a ring that matched them, but Doba had snatched it from its box at Anna's funeral and slipped it on her finger. I was glad she'd taken it, that precious reminder of her beloved cousin. The earrings were what were important to me because Anna wore them nearly every day. She'd given them to me the week before she died, and I'd last worn them at her funeral. I wondered now, as I carefully put them into my ears, if this was a special enough occasion to wear them. Except for Davey's chain and my wedding ring, they were the only good jewelry I owned.

"Hey, those belonged to Mama Anna. How come you're wearing them now?" Davey had given me a critical appraisal that made me question my decision.

"I don't know. I just felt like putting them on, if it's okay with you?" I asked, as if needing his permission.

He shrugged. "Fine with me; they look nice. Mama

Anna's dad made them for her when she was a kid. Did you know that?"

"No. When did she tell you?"

"Just did."

Another one of the many things Anna never told me about her family, like why she had left them when she did—running hard from them and hiding in her house on the hill as I now ran and hid, though from whom, I wasn't sure.

"You look pretty, Mom."

I didn't mean to look pretty, but it was nice to know I did. "Nothing special. Just going to have some coffee and talk to Mr. Richards about stuff."

"Cade?" There was a teasing twinkle in Davey's eyes. "About me?"

"Probably."

"You going to ask about his wife?" The twinkle disappeared.

Ignoring his question, I'd said, "Luna said you two were ordering a pizza and she was going to make you something special. Like cookies or something. Did she tell you that?"

"Don't do that, Mom, I'm too old for it." Annoyed, he'd left the room, slamming the door behind him. Too often I forget how quickly he has grown, even in the few weeks we'd been here. He was too old to bribe with cookies and pizza, to change the subject without answering his question. I'd talk to him later, when I got home. Be honest with him. Make it up to him.

Davey's question stayed on my mind as Cade and I

walked into Starbucks in the heat of the afternoon, but as we sat facing each other, Cade nervously sipping black coffee, me stirring sugar into an already too sweet latte, I could think of no way to tactfully bring it up. He gave me a shy, cautious smile that hinted he was afraid I might not smile back.

He was a handsome man, with looks that snuck up on you, that you didn't notice until you stared at him straight, the kind of good-looking that older women murmured about with the hint of a sly smile on their lips, recalling the fine-looking men from their youth. A woman just had to grin back at a man who looked like that, and I did.

"Those are remarkable earrings," he said, surprising me.

"Remarkable?"

He blushed, the way some men do, a half smile quickly given, quickly gone. "I mean, they're beautiful. Navajo?"

"How did you know?"

He paused, glanced down at his coffee before he answered, so I knew his answer had something to do with his wife. The last few weeks had taught me when he got that sorrowful look that lengthened his face and took all light from his eyes, it was her. I knew it because I could see it in myself, in my own eyes. "Your wife?"

"How did *you* know?" he said with just the hint of a smile, and my heart warmed. He was fighting grief like me but not for so long. But I had Davey, and I was fighting for both of us, grief and fear. "My wife was an anthropologist into Navajo culture. A couple of years ago, we were in Arizona and I bought her some earrings that looked like that, same motif, same design." He called the waitress and ordered more coffee. A grande. "Did you buy them around here?"

"They were given to me. Anna, Davey's grandmother, was Navajo." I added my newly learned tidbit. "Her father made them for her."

"Do you mind if I ask you something?" He finished most of his coffee, picked up a biscotti, put it back down.

"Depends." I was guarded.

"I don't want this . . . our meeting to turn into a grief-counseling session, but, well, I was wondering about Davey, about his father. I . . . was hoping you could tell me a little more about him, about his father's family, about the way his father died. He said something about feeling weird, that made me wonder if—"

"Wonder what?" I interrupted him, alarmed.

"About why he should feel weird. I wondered if maybe his father's death had something to do with it. When somebody you love dies violently, it puts you outside of life for a while, it's a special kind of grief, particularly for a kid, it's extremely hard to—"

"No." I gazed down the street at a couple holding hands so I wouldn't look into his eyes, but he continued as if he were pulling some painful truth from a troubled kid.

"Is he in contact with the other side of his family? You mentioned his grandmother was Navajo, so I assume his father—"

"Half African American, half Navajo."

"Well, sometimes biracial children have a tough time

coming to terms with dual cultures. You know how kids are. They like to see themselves as a whole, not half of—"

"That has nothing to do with it. He's as proud of being Navajo as he is of being black," I snapped, but the tone of my voice belied what I'd said. It wasn't race that tormented him. Without realizing I'd done it, I sighed, a long, sorry sound that carried the weight of Davey's burden and mine. How long before Davey shared his true feelings with someone else?

"Raine, I'm sorry I mentioned it. I didn't mean to upset you." He touched my hand so gently, I wouldn't have felt it if I hadn't been looking.

"No. It's okay." I took a sip of my latte, and he smiled, amused.

"Foam on your lips," he said. I grabbed a napkin to wipe it off. "Under your nose. Here, let me do it." He dabbed it off with a napkin. "Reminds me of my student teaching days with kindergartners. Always a nose to wipe, a tear to dab."

"I'll bet you were good at it," I said, and everything seemed lighter except the sorrow that crossed his eyes, and I knew he was thinking about his wife again.

"Yeah, I guess I was."

"He died in bed," I said, going back to his question and answering it with a lie because I was scared to do anything else. "My husband had—an illness—and he died in bed."

"Was it something hereditary, that Davey could be afraid he'll inherit?"

"You might say that." I avoided his eyes with a thin slice of the truth. "But we've talked about it."

"That's good."

Neither of us spoke after that, but it was a friendly silence, comfortable and easy. I closed my eyes for an instant, enjoying the sun on my face. Summer flowers—pink impatiens, red geraniums, ivies flowing to the pavement—filled large clay containers and made the space festive and relaxing, and I felt that way, too, despite the lie about Elan's death. I glanced at Cade, his thoughts elsewhere, too. Should I simply have told him the truth? But then where would the truth stop? With Davey's gift? Why we were running? I thought back to Davey wanting to know how his wife died, and Cade's joke earlier about turning this into a grief-counseling session. I studied his face with those sad, distant eyes. Maybe it would do him some good, a "counseling session." I was beyond reach; I was sure of that.

"Tell me about your wife, Denice. I can always tell when you're thinking about her because the light leaves your eyes."

"Dennie." He grinned when he said her name. "Nobody called her Denice, not even her parents."

"What was she like?"

Another grin accompanied by a faraway look in his eyes. "Can't describe her except that she was . . . well . . . you know . . . indescribable. How can you pin down someone who makes you unimaginably happy? Saved me from myself. I was a wild man before I met her. Craziness. Drugs, drink, loose women."

"Wild man?"

"Generally speaking."

"Loose women?"

"To tell the truth, I was the loose one. Nothing going for me at all."

"I can't imagine that. You strike me as a steady kind of guy, the kind everyone depends on, like Davey does, like Luna." *Like I could,* I thought but didn't say.

He leaned back in his chair, as if recalling something in his past. "Well, I can't imagine it myself these days. A lost soul, Raine, that's what I was. Spent some time in rehab for drug addiction, finally got out of that. To this day, the back of my neck crawls when a cop stares at me sideways. This was all before I was twenty-five. You never know who people are or what they've been through. How life has turned them around, how someone can teach them to save themselves."

"That's what Dennie did for you?"

"Helped me to stop lying to myself. Running from myself, from life. Just by being there, being steady. You can't hide from your fears. You face them down. Even if they're inside you. She taught me that."

I focused on the flowers behind him, the two teenagers bringing steaming coffee to their tables, anything to keep him from seeing I was a runner, a hider, too.

"Some things are impossible to face. They can kill you," I said.

I could tell my answer surprised and puzzled him. "Not if you kill it first," he said lightly, making a joke of it until that look came into his eyes again, a sigh with no sound. He took a long sip of coffee, picked up a biscotti, put it down, shrugged like he was hiding something or ashamed.

"I should probably talk about her more," he said as if

seeking some kind of wisdom or truth from me. "It won't bring her back, though. I guess that kind of loneliness is no stranger to you."

I nodded in agreement. I had no wisdom, but if the truth was what he wanted, I could tell him. "You get used to it. The loneliness."

"How?"

"You focus on the little things that make you happy. I call it the 'now' in my life, living in the present. Davey is a lot of it, sketching—I wanted to be an artist once, can you believe that?"

"I believe you could be almost anything you wanted to. But it's more than loneliness with me."

"What else?"

"It was the way she died." He shifted in his seat, moving away from me, as if what he was about to say could touch me, too. "I can't get it out of my mind. What happened to her. How brutally . . ." He couldn't finish at first, and I didn't ask him to; I knew what he would say, because I had seen it, too. I wanted to cover my ears, to keep him from saying what I knew was true but didn't. I forced myself to hear it.

After a while he found the words, but they came hard; I could tell that by the sudden haunted look in his eyes.

"They thought at first it was a break-in, then they thought *I* must have done it because there was no sign of a break-in, then that somebody she knew, that she must have let whoever did it into the house, and that wasn't like Dennie to let in somebody she didn't know. That's the thing I can't let go, that it must have been somebody she knew. It was like some animal had got to her. Pulled her apart. I can't forget it, the way I found her. I can't get it out of my mind."

His words twisted my stomach so hard I thought I would be sick. I focused my eyes on Cade, listening to what he was saying, trying to forget my last look at Elan. I wondered if my face had given anything away, but then realized he was too lost in his memories to notice.

"Sometimes when I think about it, I wonder if it was human, the thing that killed her. If it was something she conjured up from some of those crazy places her research took her, if . . . You must think *I'm* crazy for saying something like that."

"No. I don't."

"Dennie wouldn't either," he said after a minute, chuckling, saying her name bringing a smile again. "She was a person who believed that anything was possible in life, that there were more mysteries than our limited minds could comprehend . . . in life and in death, for that matter. Dennie believed in all of it."

"Like Luna?"

"Yeah, one of the many things they had in common. Nothing was out of bounds for those two, nothing. Did Luna tell you that she was the one who found us that night?"

"No," I said, remembering the way Luna's hand shook when she held the teacup, of the way she'd tried to hide it from herself as much as from me.

"They never found the killer?"

"No."

"Or clues?"

"Only thing left that I don't remember ever seeing be-

fore was this . . . artifact that must have belonged to
Dennie. She must have just bought it." Cade leaned forward, facing me now. "It must have had something to do
with her work, some kind of charm or something, but
not for good luck. At least not for Dennie."

"I think I saw it that day in the office. It looked like a
piece of a claw?"

"Yeah. Ever seen anything like that from your husband's people?"

"No," I said too quickly.

*It leaves a part of itself behind. Something to mark its vic-
tory.*

It must have been looking for us and stumbled upon
Dennie. How had it known we'd be there months before
we came? The sun was hot but I felt a stab of cold deep
within me. And that was when I saw her, coming down
the street, strolling like she had all the time in the world.
The sun picked up the blackness of her hair, the glimmer
of silver earrings in her ears. Or was it my imagination,
seeing Anna where she shouldn't be? Did she live in a
spectral world, trying to warn me like she always had,
even from her grave?

"I need to go home," I said too loudly, too abruptly.

Cade's surprised glance turned apologetic. "I'm sorry,
scaring you with all this craziness. Raine, I . . . was looking forward to spending this time with you. . . ."

The catch in his voice, the tenderness held me, soft-
ening my fear. "Cade . . . I . . ."

"Please. It's been so long since I've talked to anybody
about anything. Other teachers don't want to hear it.
My friends—our old friends, mine and Dennie's—seem

to have quietly disappeared. Luna, well, talking about Dennie tears her apart, too. Would you believe this is the first time I've been out, sat down over coffee with a friend just to talk since Dennie died? Pathetic, isn't it?"

I looked to where she'd been, but the woman was gone. Maybe she had never been. A smile came to my lips, albeit a reluctant one. His words had come easily and without thought, and there was kindness in both his eyes and voice. Except for Mack, who was nearly as old as my grandfather, no man had spoken to me with such warmth in a long time. Too often there was a smack of lewdness to the remarks, an awkward request for a date, unwelcome comments about my appearance. A real date? I hadn't been on a date once since Elan's death. And this was a date, I realized. Despite what both of us had thought.

"It's been eleven years for me," I said. "To really talk about . . . things that are important. To listen to someone else. Eleven years. Now, *that's* pathetic!" We both laughed at that, self-consciously, and I remembered how easy it had been to laugh with him that first day in his kitchen, and I'd hardly known him then. There had been an ease between us that I assumed came from Davey's presence; I knew now it was more.

"But why so long? You're such a beautiful woman, Raine."

"Well . . . I don't know. I guess . . . I'm not that beautiful to everybody."

"Now, I can't believe that!"

"And I can't believe that you were once a wild man!"

"I'll have to show you pictures sometime. Me bummed

out on weed, bourbon." He glanced down again, the glimmer of something I couldn't read in his eyes.

"I guess a lot of my being alone is my own fault. I've been . . . trying to raise Davey on my own. It's hard being a single mom. Traveling so much." I hadn't meant to let that slip out, but it had.

"A lot of the kids in my class have parents who are divorced or separated, but they still get out, go on dates. But they don't travel. I know I'm getting into dangerous territory here, but to be honest, I've been wondering about that, why you don't stay in one place. Do you think Davey's okay with it?"

"He's fine," I said quickly. Too quickly.

"Every time I ask him something about school next year, he won't look me in the eye. Maybe he thinks he's weird because he hasn't been anyplace long enough to put down roots."

"You *are* in dangerous territory," I said, biting the biscotti so I wouldn't have to say more.

He nodded as if he understood. "Maybe another time we can talk about that? Maybe over dinner or something?"

"Yeah." I wished it were true, that it would be as simple as that, to meet a man like Cade, go out for dinner and a drink, forget everything that I'd been living. Maybe there was that chance once. But not now. "I need to be getting back to Luna's. She's watching Davey, and—"

"More dangerous territory," he said, half-joking. "Davey is eleven. He's really old enough to watch himself. Maybe he needs to be on his own more. You don't want to overprotect him. Boys need room—believe me, I know."

"Yeah." Half an answer because I heard him but hadn't. We finished up our coffee slowly, and as we headed out, Cade touched my hand again in the gentle way he had, and I felt something else, too, a tingling inside me, like I'd felt when Elan touched me that first time. How could that be so? Should I let myself feel it?

"Dinner? No Davey? No Luna, just us?"

"Okay," I said, but my heart was beating fast because I was admitting to myself for the first time since I'd been here, how attracted I was to him, and that I knew he felt the same. I could see it in his eyes, shy yet strangely bold, and the way he touched me when he really didn't need to. Things had changed between us, subtly but certainly, and I wasn't sure where they would go from here. It was time for the "now" moments I allowed myself, with this man in a Starbucks, of all places, and if nothing else happened between us, I could look back on this day for as long as I needed to.

"Ready to go." He offered his hand, and I took it, aware of the feel of it, the softness of his palm, the mild shock that wasn't one, the "electricity" they talk about in love songs. I let myself enjoy it, the intertwining of our fingers that neither of us expected.

It was then that I heard it. The sound of its paws on the sidewalk. *Plop. Plop. Plop.* It came closer. Next to the flowerpots, nearer to our table. Past the teenagers with their coffee, stopping to sniff the air. I held Cade's hand tight, closed my eyes, wanting to make it disappear. But it was upon us before I knew it. Nuzzling. Pushing its way between us. Licking my hand that was free.

I screamed, snatched my hand from its jaws, brought it close to my breast.

Cade held my other hand, leaned toward me, whispering, "Raine. It's just a dog!"

"No!"

"Raine, look." He bent down, and it turned toward him, ignoring me. He whistled low between his teeth, calling it toward him like it was a pet, and the thing looked up at him as Cade stroked its fur. It licked his hand, but turned its eyes toward me.

"Look, he's friendly," Cade said, and I wanted him to be right that it was just a dog. A stray escaped from someone's yard. It was acting that way, trotting around in a circle, waiting to be petted or scratched behind its ears. A black Labrador, big enough to stand on its hind legs and reach your throat.

"Don't touch it!" I said, still afraid, but Cade ignored me.

"Probably a stray. Could be that dog that was doing so much howling the other night. Did Davey mention it to you? It scared him, he said."

I let Cade's hand go and stepped away from him and from it, searching for what I knew was there.

Something doesn't come back like it should, a nose looks like a snout, all wet and thick and nasty; an eye bigger than it should be that can't be kept closed, claws tipping fingers instead of nails, something will tell you, but you got to see it, Raine, and when you do, take that boy and run for all you're worth. Don't leave a clue behind.

It was the eyes this time. Yellow. Strangely human but

dead and empty, pupils round and black, with no expression, like looking into death itself. It went for my hand, quick and fierce like an animal would, white teeth sharp and needle thin, bending backwards—a shark's teeth made for ripping and tearing.

Protecting me, Cade jumped in its way, and it backed away. Startled, it growled, gazed around the space, sniffing behind me. It was looking for Davey, but it was waiting its time, patiently like always. And then it turned, nice dog again, sat at Cade's feet as if he were its master, and that frightened me more than anything I could think of.

Yet Cade was as surprised as me. "Go! Get out of here!" he yelled, stepping in front of me.

And it whined as if wounded and slunk away, tail between its legs. I didn't realize I was shaking until Cade pulled me close to him, and I felt my trembling body against his strong one.

"Hey, Raine. You okay?" I nodded that I was, but my head barely moved. "I'll call animal control when I get home and have it picked up. It's a stray. Probably harmless, but it shouldn't have gone after you like it did. Hey—"

I was shaking so hard, I couldn't talk.

"Calm down! It's over. The dog is gone." He hugged me and I let myself fit into his body, safe.

"I need to leave," I said.

Neither of us spoke on the way home. Him, puzzled by my actions, and me, lost in thoughts I couldn't share.

8

cade

It was early when Cade dropped Raine off at Luna's, and he didn't know what to do with himself; her presence wouldn't leave him. Luna had asked if he wanted to come in, sit around, have some tea, but he refused. He didn't want to lose the feeling Raine had left him with, that touch of teenage giddiness he hadn't felt since Dennie died. He wanted the afternoon to stay untouched in his mind, let it linger as long as it could. But when he came into his house—into its loneliness and silence—he wondered if he should have taken Luna up on her offer—sat awhile, chatted about nothing, made sure Raine was okay, even though the closer to home they'd gotten, the stronger she seemed. He was still puzzled by her reaction to the dog, the trembling that overtook her.

He hoped he hadn't made a fool of himself, begging her to stay and talk as he had, despite her obvious discomfort. He'd been more concerned with his own feelings than with hers, which must have been clear to her, too. Yet she sat and listened, every word he spoke seeming to touch her as deeply as they once had Dennie. She listened like Dennie, too, all heart and eyes. He never thought anyone could hear him like that again, as if every word stuck in some pocket of her soul. That damn stray had sure shaken her up, though—both her and the boy must be terrified of dogs—and the way the dog snapped at her hands, close to nipping her fingers, had scared him, too. Damn filthy mutt. At some point, he'd ask her why she was so frightened, maybe when they went out again. On the way home, she'd mentioned a movie she wanted to see, and maybe they'd catch it one Sunday. Just thinking about the possibility made him grin.

He called animal control as he promised he would, and after leaving a message about a stray dog that might be vicious, sat down at the kitchen table acutely aware of his aloneness. He considered pouring a drink, then changed his mind. Recalling Raine's words about not being able to imagine him as the wild man he had been made him chuckle in wonder. Wild man and more, that was the truth of it. Not giving a damn about life, love, or limb. Booze, weed, blow—anything he could drink, smoke, or snort to send him into oblivion.

He couldn't remember those days without a burning sense of shame and embarrassment. He'd even dealt drugs for a hot minute when he dropped out of college. Light stuff mostly, weed, no weight. It was sheer luck and good timing that had kept him out of jail; a dozen times he could have landed there easy enough. Hell, the cops knew he was dealing, but he was too slick to get caught. To this day, there were cops out there who still had it in for him, and if he hadn't been at work the day Dennie was murdered, they would have pinned that on him, just out of spite. God, he'd been so young and cocky—nothing could touch him. Even his old man's death wasn't enough to stop him from drinking, even when the insurance money got him back in school. One snowy night he'd run his truck off Route 17, damn near killed himself. Lucky for him, he'd been sober enough to make it home. Then he'd met Dennie with her serious, trusting, studious self. It had scared him how closely and quickly she drew him to her.

He'd put up a fight at first, running as fast as he could, back to the women who followed him around, panties falling around their ankles, and he smiled for an instant, remembering how Raine had laughed at the words he so thoughtlessly used to describe them. Loose women? What kind of bullshit was that? Like he'd said, *he* was the loose one. Three quarters of them had tender hearts he'd taken no time breaking. To this day, he was half-scared he'd run into some woman with a .45 tucked in her bag, determined to shoot him dead for being such a coldhearted son of a bitch. He'd been terrified he'd find some way to hurt Dennie, too, bring her to her knees, down to his level, but cautiously, effortlessly, she had pulled him up to hers.

He was afraid of Raine the same way, yet it wasn't wildness but grief he feared would touch her. Better for her to leave him alone, let him wallow in his sorry life. Let him come home. Correct some papers. Get drunk. Watch TV. Fall asleep on the couch like he'd been doing for the past year. How could he pull a woman with a vulnerable kid into the dark smelly world he inhabited?

Yet there was still that glimmer of hope, the one even

sorrow couldn't snuff out, that Dennie had left burning in his heart. Let her pull you into her world, she would say. Let her pull you into her world like I did.

But what kind of world did Raine live in?

Some things are impossible to face. They can kill you.

What had happened to make her so wary, so frightened of life? Was it—or some man—still tied to her? Could she ever trust him enough to tell him the truth? Why was she still alone after so many years? Surely she was joking or exaggerating just to make him feel better about his own loneliness. It made no sense for a woman with a smile like hers, which could pull you out of your own sorry funk against your will. How could those restless, haunting eyes not have enchanted some man by now? Her son had them, too, those eyes. Angel eyes, he'd heard them called—that peeked inside you and saw the slice of heaven—or hell—that lay there.

You focus on the little things that make you happy. I call it the "now" in my life. Davey is a lot of it, drawing—I wanted to be an artist once, can you believe that?

He was willing to believe anything she told him, he realized, and maybe he should focus on his "now" as she did hers. But what exactly was his "now"? He only hoped he hadn't scared her with all that mess about something inhuman killing Dennie, but God help him, that was what he believed. Only Luna knew what he'd seen, because she'd been there. Neither of them had spoken of it since. What he told his coworkers had been sanitized, and although they knew *he* didn't kill her, there was still a subtle mistrust, a vague suspicion in their eyes that he, through carelessness or neglect, had brought this hell upon himself. He'd even begun to wonder if he *was* being punished for his past. Yet Raine had listened to him as if he were making sense, accepting without question or suspicion what he said.

Strangely enough, foolishly enough, he'd had misgivings about a date with a woman other than Dennie, despite all the women he'd been with—been through—in the past. When he was with Dennie, he'd never looked at anyone else. Well, maybe looked, but certainly never touched. Never felt the feelings that brewed inside him when he touched Raine that first time. Just a touch. A tingling like a gentle shock shooting straight down his loins that told him he'd been away from women too damn long. Could just touching a woman make him feel like that? Did she feel it, what he had felt?

He felt guilty, then heard Dennie's voice the way he could if he listened to the silence in the house, to the space inside his head.

How long do you plan to put yourself through this?

Until I'm through.

I'm dead, my darling, let me go!

Could those be her words, her voice? If only he could hear it again, once more before he died.

He felt like a drink again, like getting drunk out of his skull, but he couldn't. Proving something to Raine, that he wasn't that man he'd once been, that she believed he could never have been?

What the hell was he thinking? He hardly knew the woman!

Now, I can't believe that, that you were once a wild man.

Prove himself to whom? To himself, to Dennie?

He put on the kettle to make himself some tea. In honor of Luna. How often had he and Dennie joked about that—in honor of Luna—when she spooned chamomile leaves into the teapot and filled it with boiling water? They would settle down on the couch, sipping tea sweet with honey that smelled of flowers, download some mindless flick from Netflix, then slip into bed and make love.

To hear her voice again. Just once.

He remembered the digital recorder he hadn't set eyes on since her death. Turning off the kettle, he put the cup and teapot—a dainty blue one Luna had given them—back into the cupboard and snapped on the light in Dennie's study. Everything rushed back—Davey screaming, running like the devil was chasing him, Raine dashing after him, Luna taking the whole scene in, watching, listening, saying nothing. Despite it all, he forced himself into the room to the desk and went through her papers, studying, but just for an instant, their wedding photo. The digital recorder was in a plastic bag in the desk drawer, near the thing that gave him the creeps. He felt a sense of dread as he pushed it aside, grabbed the bag, careful not to touch it.

Dennie had always been a meticulous researcher. Some of the recordings had already been transcribed, and he knew if he looked through the folders, he'd find each labeled with the time and date of transcription. He used to tease her about it, how carefully she recorded and labeled things, to which she would tell him, as serious about this as she was about everything else, that she was a scientist, too, solving mysteries others thought unsolvable. He picked up the digital recorder—the most expensive he could find when he'd bought it, replacing the fifty-dollar piece of junk she'd used since grad school—loaded it with new batteries, and took it back into the kitchen, quickly closing the office door, like something might get out, he thought, then laughed at his own foolishness. He pulled his laptop out of his briefcase, and plugged the recorder into a USB slot.

Was he ready for this? What good was her voice without her to speak it? Better to give the damn thing to her advisor with the rest of her papers. Let somebody who didn't love her listen to her voice. Yet even as he thought it, he knew he could never let the recorder go, not with a piece of her inside. He couldn't take the chance that he might wake one morning and not be able to recall her voice, so low and just this side of sultry, always hiding a chuckle begging to break out.

He chose a day at random. July 6—his birthday. He hadn't bothered to celebrate it this year, hadn't remembered until it was over. So this would be a belated gift to himself—the sound of Dennie's voice. Putting on earphones, he closed his eyes, turned on the recorder, and there she was, as close and clear as if she were sitting across from him. *Notes . . .* , she began, then stopped and giggled. The sound of that girlish, flighty laughter tore at his heart. He didn't think he could continue, but then came her voice, solid and soft, followed by his own, and he remembered that afternoon in all its color and high spirits.

He'd come home early from work that day, found her in her study, notebook open, recording something for further investigation. She did that sometimes, recorded reminders to herself. Easier than writing, she said, her thoughts came easily. What was she laughing at? Him? He listened to his own footsteps entering the room.

What are you *doing home?*

Getting in your way.

It may be your birthday . . . but . . .

More laughter. He'd grabbed her, kissed her, teasing her lips with his tongue. He remembered the softness of her skin, the tenderness of that kiss.

Early birthday present.

Down payment?

Promise?

Okay, let me finish this first. Her professorial voice took over, the one that spoke so authoritatively to her students, dictated comments for her dissertation, interviewed subjects. He'd left and gone into the kitchen to correct homework.

He cut it off. Rewound to the voices. Found the laughter, playing it over and over again, and then, finally, came to what happened next: an interview with an expert on Navajo witchcraft, research from some famous anthropologist, Clyde Kluckhohn, whose work she admired. He skipped to another date, two days later. Notes from research by scholars and cultural anthropologists even he recognized: Margaret Mead, Claude Lévi-Strauss, Zora Neale Hurston. If Dennie had lived, she would have been one of the great ones. If Dennie had lived . . . He turned off the recorder, but still her voice lingered, inside the folds of the curtains, the plaster in the walls, within his mind.

The bottle of bourbon sat patiently waiting for him in

the kitchen cabinet. He could see it, smell it, taste it even, something to ease the trembling that had come over him as violently as Raine had shook when that damn dog nipped at her hand. Raine. It wasn't like he'd promised her anything—but her words came back.

You strike me as the kind of guy everyone depends on, like Luna, like Davey does.

How long had it been since anyone depended on him? He put it from his mind, that bottle of Jim Beam. Jimmy B, his daddy used to call it in disgust, because he wouldn't touch it. The memory of that and his father made him wince. No. At least not for tonight.

He placed his laptop, digital recorder still attached, in his briefcase and pushed it underneath the desk in the living room, where he corrected papers. (Dennie had the *real* office; they'd decided that when they bought the house.) He got out the pasta salad he'd bought a couple of days ago, sniffed it to make sure it wasn't spoiled, then pulled out what was left of the rotisserie chicken he'd bought yesterday at ShopRite. Good enough for tonight.

The doorbell rang as he was pulling off a chicken leg. Raine was his first thought, and he wondered why. He'd just left her, after all, what could she want . . . except it was he, he had to admit to himself, who wanted to see her. Thinking of her put a smile on his face even though he knew it was probably Luna come to check on him, always looking out for him, bringing some food. So much for leftovers.

His smile dropped abruptly when he opened the door and saw who it was. Forgotten feelings came back then:

how he felt about cops, the memory of himself in those days.

"Cade Richards?" The old one spoke first. He looked like death turned over twice, acne-scarred skin dotted with flesh moles, a voice scratchy and deep, the kind that came from smoking too many Lucky Strikes when you could find them. Cade tried to place his face but couldn't; he'd remember a face and voice like that.

"Good evening, Officers. How can I help you?" His voice was the formal one, schoolboy neat and proper, the one he'd pulled out when he spoke to the police all those years back.

"Can we step in?" There were two of them. The junior partner was losing his hair, too young for that, Cade thought. He stepped back, knew better than not to. The two stepped inside, peering around like cops did in unfamiliar places. Cade's hair crept up the back of his neck.

"How can I help you?" Same tone, overly formal, calm but Cade knew something was up, something to do with Dennie.

Had they found out who killed her?

"Just a question or two." The other one spoke. He was younger than Cade, late twenties, nervous. He glanced toward Dennie's office and swiftly brought his gaze back to Cade, who knew then that this one had been in the house before, the day Dennie died. "There was a murder across town, last night. Restaurant owner, Walter Mack. Do you know him?"

So they hadn't found out anything new, after all.

Cade's stomach dropped. He couldn't make himself respond to the question.

"He was . . . uh . . . well . . . uh . . . murdered in a manner that closely resembled how your wife was . . . murdered." *Brutalized. Mutilated. Desecrated.* Cade knew what he meant. Nobody could walk into a scene like the one in that study and not have it seared into his memory forever or easily find words to describe it. "We wondered if there was any chance that you or your late wife knew him, were acquainted with him?"

"The same way?" Cade felt sick. It took him a while to find his voice.

"Yeah." The young cop looked at the floor, avoiding his eyes.

"When?"

"Last night." Cade realized they'd told him that before.

"Walter Mack? No. I don't know him. Never heard of him."

"Can you think of any way that the two of them . . . your wife and the deceased, could be connected? Anyone they knew or had in common?"

"No . . . I don't think so. I'm sure, no."

"Absolutely sure?" The older one had taken over the questioning now, his eyes suspiciously focused on Cade as if he could squeeze out the truth if he stared at him long enough.

"Yes." Cade made his voice firm, unequivocal. Without saying anything else, the older one handed him his card, and Cade wondered, foolishly, if they had given him a card that night, if they had bothered.

"If you can think of anybody, anything that connects them—Mr. Mack and your wife—please call me." Cade nodded, took the card, shoved it into his pocket. He watched them walk down to the sidewalk, climb into a black Ford sedan, drive away.

Only then did he get down the bottle of Jim Beam that waited for him, pour himself a full glass, gulp it down quickly, pour another, and then call the one person in the world who might know more than he did.

9

raine

Mack had been dead three weeks before Davey and I found out. There had been no reason for Cade or Luna to mention it, since I never told them about Mack, my job, or how much we loved him. The thing about secrets is that you couldn't stop keeping them. They held you tight, even when you wanted to break loose. Mack was one crooked piece that didn't quite fit into my puzzle, part of our secret life nobody knew about, and I ended up paying for it. When Luna told me about her talk with Cade the night the cops came, she mentioned it only because she was concerned he was drinking again, and it worried her. She didn't give any of the details.

Cade and I had been out a lot since that first date—for coffee, to see movies, mostly just to walk and talk. I knew he still struggled with the urge to "drown his sorrows," as he jokingly put it. He'd mentioned it one night after a movie when I had a glass of wine and he had black coffee despite the hour. He was staying away from alcohol because he'd drunk more than he should have a couple of weeks ago, he'd said, and when I asked him why, he told me because he'd been sad and scared. Are you sad and scared a lot? I'd asked, curious about what he wasn't telling me, and he'd smiled that shy, hesitant way he had, and said not as much as he used to be, thanks to me. Thanks to me and Davey, that old bottle of Jim Beam had been untouched since then. You make me happy, Raine, he said, and I haven't been happy since Dennie died.

That was true for me, too, but I wasn't ready to tell him yet; I was afraid of what might happen. When he kissed me that night, it was not the gentle touch I was used to, but a full-hearted passionate kiss—a lover's kiss—that went straight down my spine.

We often held hands, cautiously at first, which added to the sweetness, like kids on the run, scared of letting go or getting caught, and that's what we were in a way—scared of what was chasing us finally catching up. Sitting in dark, close theaters, chomping popcorn, sipping Cokes, walking to Starbucks for an iced latte late in the day. I had begun to feel like everything was normal, okay. Davey had grown to trust Cade, and grew closer each time they were together. He was hoping for normal, too, even if it was only for a couple of hours every day. Neither of us had seen or sensed Anna, if that's what that fleeting, elusive vision had been. And the dog? I'd decided it just might be a stray, like Cade said. Funny how your heart could put your mind under a spell.

His deep, tender kisses had begun to ignite feelings unfelt since Elan's death, and when I'd close my eyes at night, I'd imagine Cade lying beside me, his lips and fingers caressing my breasts and parts of myself that I once allowed to enjoy such feelings. And I'd think about how I'd kiss his lips, so full and sensual, the corners of them turning up just the slightest bit, even when he frowned. I'd imagine how it would be to draw close to him, feel him lying strong beside me, helping me keep us safe from harm. Those tender places I'd only allowed Elan to know, to touch—were awakening again. It was the same for him; I knew that, too.

But Mack dying like he did for the reason he had, ripped all that foolishness to shreds.

The morning I found out had started peacefully enough—Luna frying bacon for breakfast, baking buttermilk biscuits for Davey. She'd just put them in the oven when Davey screamed—once, twice—not like a kid does but a painful, woeful cry that tore straight from his throat. He was clutching the morning paper to his chest, and I snatched it from his arms when I saw what was in it. It was about Mack, and how they were still looking for the murderer who had killed him three weeks ago. They suspected it must have been someone close—a family member, spurned lover, angry partner—because of the violence inflicted upon his body and the nature of his wounds. I knew what that meant. So did Davey.

"It got him, it got Mr. Mack like it did Cade's wife, like it killed my dad." Davey's voice faded into a low, bitter whisper. I was used to Davey crying, screaming in fear even, but I'd never heard that tone before, coming from somewhere I didn't know.

Walter Mack, sixty-two, had been "hacked" beyond recognition, the paper said. Hacked was wrong; if it did what had been done to Dennie, to Elan, that was beyond any word the cops or papers could come up with. When Davey screamed, Luna rushed into the living room, biscuit dough on fingers, flour dotting her face. She picked the paper off the floor and quickly read it.

"Raine, did you know this man?" Her eyes were wide, frightened. I nodded, too stunned to speak. "Is he connected to . . . the boy's family? To Anna?"

"No." Finding my voice, I glanced at Davey, who had settled on the couch, staring straight ahead. I knew he was trying to keep his body under control. I could see him struggle, and I turned my head, giving him the space he needed to find and settle back into himself. "I worked for Mack. In his restaurant, before we came here. He was my friend . . . Davey's friend."

"More than a friend!" Davey's voice was hoarse from the scream. "You know that, Mom, that he was more than just a friend!" Luna shot me a look, her eyes nearly as wide as his.

"How long had you worked for him?"

"Most of the time we were here. Mack called me at the beginning of the summer. I didn't call him back. . . ." My voice faded with shame and guilt.

"You didn't call him back! You didn't tell me?" Davey screamed, out of control again, but there was nothing I could say; I had no excuse. I took the paper from Luna, unfolded and studied it because I didn't want to look into my son's face and see the accusation in his eyes.

It was an old photograph, one Mack's wife had taken years before she died, one he had always been proud of, but the years had changed him. It looked nothing like him now, which was why he said he loved it, though he still had that quick grin, eager for a prank or joke, eyes that gleamed with good humor. He was a thin man with a bony face and a head, always clean-shaven, that seemed to take up more of him than it should have. He was too slight to have put up much of a fight.

The paper must have gotten the photograph from one of his kids. No grandchildren, which was why he used to say he felt so close to Davey. Stepgrandson, he used to call him. Davey called him Mr. Mack, and he was the closest thing to a grandfather he would ever know. I was grateful for that.

Luna's gaze switched away from Davey and back to me. I sensed there was something she would tell me later because she didn't want him to hear it.

"You don't know that," she said. "You don't know how Mack died. It could have been somebody who hated him, like the paper said. All you know about Mack's life was what he let you see. It could have been someone from years back. Don't take it on yourself like that. Don't—"

"I know what it was, Luna." There was a fierceness in his voice, in the way he held his body that I'd never seen or heard before. Luna sat down beside him on the couch, put her arm around him, yet barely touched, giving him the space she sensed he needed.

"He's gone," she said so softly, I barely heard her. "Don't think about how he died. Just remember what you loved about him. About the gift he gave you."

"I know how he died." Davey's eyes brimmed with anger. "I owe him."

"Owe?" I said, troubled by the tone of his voice, the rage in his eyes.

"Owe. Because Mr. Mack was my friend." He glared at me, daring me to defy him, a half smile forming on his lips. "Don't worry, Mom. I'm not ready yet, but I will be soon." Those were Anna's words, speaking of revenge for blood sins, Anna's voice coming out of the mouth of my eleven-year-old boy, and they chilled me because I knew what they meant. I'd tried to forget he would ever say them, and they reminded me that she and Elan were half of him the same as me, and I would never fully understand what dwelled inside him. Someday he would be ready, like Anna said he would, to become that creature that could fight, take revenge on what had killed his father and his friend and what always threatened us. He was months away from adolescence, and those words, so firmly spoken, filled the room with tension and my fear.

"You're a kid," Luna said, brushing his words aside and breaking the mood. "Someday it will be your fight, but not today."

"Then when?" Davey stood up, backing away from both of us, and I noticed not for the first time just how much he had grown in three months, shaping into a teenager, not the boy I knew. Some of it was the influence of Cade, the impact of a grown man on the life of a boy whose father is gone, and I realized again how much my son had missed Mack, how essential he must have been to Davey in ways I never fully realized.

"When the time is right, you'll know it," Luna said. "And so will your mom."

I warned her with my eyes not to go on with this, feed

into whatever he was feeling, but she shot me a look that said, Leave it alone, let it be for now, okay? Without answering, Davey walked upstairs, his foot heavy on every stair, slamming the door to his room.

Luna and I didn't speak for a good five minutes after he had gone. "Breakfast is ready, but this is definitely not the time to talk about biscuits," she said grimly. The irrelevance of breakfast and her words, delivered with such deadpan irony, made me laugh and just as suddenly cry, tears rolling down my face as I remembered Mack, thought about Davey and the battle he was so determined to wage.

Don't trust nobody. Not family. Not friend. Don't let it get him like it got my son, not until he is ready to meet it. And remember that blood must pay for blood. A debt must be paid. Your boy can never forget. That is his destiny.

Anna's words, taunting me as they had every day since she left us.

"I can see the change in him, too." Luna broke into my thoughts, her expression as somber as her words. "I've seen it for some time. You know he's not going to let you run away this time. You've got to come up with something else or he will."

"I need more time, Luna. He needs more time to grow into whatever . . ." I couldn't finish the sentence, because I didn't know what it was. The thing that killed his father? Dennie? Mack? And in that moment, I thought of Cade, how he would view Davey when he found out that the "weird" part of himself had been planted inside along with his beautiful eyes; it was as much a part of him as the smart, funny kid who loved to play chess. "I don't have a choice, Luna. I have to go. I can't face—"

"Face what?" Annoyance creased the space between Luna's eyes in a tight line. "Yourself? Davey? Cade?"

I didn't answer, and the air again grew heavy with her doubts and my secrets.

"You're family, Raine," Luna said after a moment. "No matter what. You're blood, and Mama told me to look out for you. That's why she carried on about that church like she did. She knew you needed family."

"What about Davey?"

"You know better than to ask me something like that. At this point, you two are the only family I've got."

"But we've got to leave, Luna."

"He'll have something to say about that," she said, nodding toward the stairs.

She was right, and I went back to my own thoughts, trying to figure out how I could explain to Davey that we had no choice but to go; that he wasn't ready for whatever fight Anna had been talking about, wouldn't be for years, even Anna would know that. As far as things went with Cade, it would be best to slip away as quietly as we'd come. Drop out of his life as quickly as we'd dropped in.

I thought about what he'd said yesterday, about me making him happier than he'd been since Dennie died, and how I'd be leaving him like I left Mack and half the other people who had welcomed me into their lives, without a good-bye or backward glance.

"What choice do I have?" I said as much to myself as to Luna.

Luna scowled, with frustration or anger, I couldn't tell which. "To tell the truth, Raine, I don't know. This one is on you. But I'll tell you this: Whatever the hell you do, stay or leave, you've got to do it soon. You don't have much time."

There was urgency in her voice and the way she couldn't quite look at me puzzled and alarmed me. I was learning Luna's ways, and she could be as inscrutable and balky about things she knew and didn't want you to know as Anna had been. Sometimes it was amusing, almost endearing. Occasionally it got on my nerves; this was one of those times, and I didn't hide my irritation.

"What are you talking about? You hide so many things, Luna. You don't tell the whole truth, or everything you know. What the hell are you talking about?" Suddenly I was as angry as Davey had been when he stomped up to his room—about Mack, Davey, Cade, everything that was coming to a head—and my rage had nowhere to go; Luna was the closest target. "Why don't you say what you mean? You've never told me what I needed to know about Cade, about the way his wife died, about the impact it could have on us. I told you about Davey and you knew about his wife, yet you sat there, sipping your goddamn tea, burning your incense, not saying a goddamn thing!"

"Raine—"

"And don't say it wasn't your place! Don't tell me that again. You knew what was going on. You're like some master manipulator—throwing us together, watching things spark, and then keeping what we really need to know about each other's secret. Who are you really, Luna? What kind of woman are you." I was on my feet then, screaming like a kid waiting for a parent to put her in her place, say something, answer my accusations.

Luna studied me for a minute, then opened a drawer in the coffee table in front of the couch, pulled out an ivory case containing Marlboro Lights, and lit one. "Told Mama I would give these things up before she died, but I kept a few just in case," she said as sweetly as if she hadn't heard a word I said. "You're right, Raine. Right as rain, huh?"

"Cut it out!"

"Listen to me, and I'll tell you the truth."

"Do you even *know* the truth?" I said, so angry at her, I couldn't bear to look in her direction.

"Yeah, I know it—more than I should, half the time—and I'm never sure what's real and what's not. That comes with the territory of my mind, the same way Davey has to deal with his 'gift,' if that's what it's called. I've got to deal with mine, and half the time, it's more a pain in the ass than a boon, which is what your aunt Geneva used to call it. Ask your son about his. That's one thing Davey and I have in common."

A strong bond had developed between the two of them in the past few months; she was telling the truth about that. I could see it in the easy, comfortable way they were with each other, how easily they talked and laughed. Like he'd been with Anna, a connection I would never have.

"Shit comes in and out of my head from no particular place. The thing about folks like me and Davey is that we have no idea what to do with what comes and goes. Davey's is physical, with his body and soul. Mine is in my head, which explodes more times than I care to say. So what I *do* say is only what I know. In black-and-white, what I know to be absolutely, undeniably true."

I gave her a reluctant nod of acknowledgment because I understood some of what she was saying, about herself and our family, too. We were a family of secrets, and secrets never did anyone much good.

"I don't *really* know what killed Dennie or Mack or Elan or what is after you. What I do know is that you and Cade need each other, that you will be each other's salvation, but I don't know why." She gave a short, quick laugh, almost a chuckle, and pulled in smoke from her cigarette, blowing it out easy and slow. "I used to get so disgusted with Mama when she would only tell me bits and pieces because she said she didn't know, and now I understand. I'll tell you something else I know—moons."

"Moons!" Why had she thrown that in? Was she joking? Her eyes, shy yet defensive, told me she wasn't.

"You've watched enough TV to know the connection between wolves and full moons." She gave a lighthearted shrug that I chose to ignore. "Anybody who catches a few episodes of *True Blood* or *Supernatural* can tell you that. But I know the truth about the evil things that roam this Earth, and I know their power can come and go with the strength of the moon. Like that damn dog that sniffs around here—"

"You've seen it!"

"Once or twice."

"When was the last time?" I asked, but I knew before

she answered. Three weeks ago, when Mack died. It must have been looking for Davey.

"There are things that are as old as Earth—both good and evil—almost as old as when the moon pulled itself away. Maybe that's why wolves howl at a full moon, why folks go crazy and babies get born. Mama named me Luna because of that moon, maybe that's why she pulled you to me."

"It will be back, then—for Davey, for me."

"For Davey. It was never about you. I'm sure of that. Full moons always bring things out, unleash that part of creatures they can't control. It may not have set out to kill Mack or Dennie, but it did. Dennie was killed during the day, but that night, the moon was full. Mack? It was as big as a pumpkin. I remember thinking that someone close was going to die."

"So how much time do I have?" I said more to myself than to Luna. How much time to say any good-byes I had to say, talk to Davey, make him understand.

"About a week." Luna's tone was matter-of-fact, but I could see the anguish in her eyes. "There are two full moons in August. The first when it got Mack, the next at the end. Blue moon, they call it. Last day. That's how much time you've got, Raine, so if you're going to go, you best be gone by then."

Regret and weariness weighed down her voice and body. Things had changed from that first day when she seemed sure that she could help me find a way to stay. Mack's death, seeing what the thing had left, maybe remembering again how Dennie had died. Luna no longer believed we could beat it; her face was empty of answers.

"You got to find a way to save Davey, too. If you don't, he'll grow into the thing that's chasing him. You got to find a way to give him back his life without taking it."

Her words stung me. I couldn't speak, because I knew they were true. We sat there, and Luna sighed like she does sometimes, but heavier than usual, hopeless.

When Davey came down, I wondered if he had heard us talking, but couldn't bring myself to ask. Maybe Davey knew what was up, maybe he didn't, but he didn't say anything, and I knew he felt bad about how he'd left earlier. Luna went back into the kitchen and put the biscuits on and we had breakfast. Nobody spoke; nobody ate much. When we'd finished, Luna went to watch one of her Discovery Channel programs, Davey to finish some homework for Cade. I sat in the backyard, feverishly drawing the bushes where the lilacs had bloomed.

Later that day, Cade called and asked if Davey and I would like to go to a street carnival in the next town. It was funny when I thought about it, something so commonplace, so normal—yet neither Davey nor I had ever been to one. Yeah, I said, I'd love to go. It will be fun, he told me. For me it would be a chance to find a way to say good-bye, to let him know how much he'd meant to us. It would be the last time we would be together. I knew that, too.

And before I slept, I remembered the fantasies I'd had about him, how much I'd wanted him to touch me, to feel him inside me, but that would never happen. That dream was as dead and gone as the grin of Walter Mack, whose torn, featureless face wouldn't leave my mind.

10

raine

"I'm not leaving," Davey said first thing next morning, then chanced a look at Luna to see if she would offer any support. She threw him a glance that said leave me out of this, and beat a hasty retreat out of the kitchen. I knew she hadn't had time to mention my plans to Davey, but he knew me well enough to guess my next move. "You can go if you want to, but I'm not," he said, making his point again.

It was hot in the room, and the bright green Luna had painted the kitchen walls added to the heat. I'd gotten used to Luna's color schemes: the turquoises springing from nowhere, the calm beiges littered with dots of pink and maroon. And green. Luna claimed green made her feel cool because it reminded her of trees; it wasn't working for me this morning. The air conditioner had broken the week before, and the squeaky ceiling fan over the kitchen table was doing double duty. I didn't feel like fighting. Up until recently, my arguments with Davey had been laced with touches of humor, but that had recently changed, right along with the tinted glasses that in mid-July replaced his Harry Potter glasses and the blue skullcap with the Nets logo pulled low and hiding his hair, which he'd taken to wearing despite the summer's heat.

"You know that's not going to work." My voice was as calm as I could make it as I sipped my coffee. "Where do you think you're going to live?"

"I can take care of myself. Mama Anna told me I'd have to someday, and she told me how to do it."

"Is that so." I casually scanned the morning paper, but his defiance had set me on edge. Anna and Elan were in him, too, and those parts were crowding me out, making themselves known. Mack's death had done it, and his anger that we were leaving . . . again.

"What did she tell you?" I asked cautiously. I rarely asked him about his talks with Anna, though I knew she still had power over him, even from her grave. "Did she tell you where to go when you change, did she tell you where to hide?"

He looked straight ahead, his face hardening.

"What did she say?"

"Secret," he said.

The thing about folks like me and Davey is that we have no idea what to do with what comes and goes.

I didn't know how to help him.

I would try later, when we got back from the street fair. I'd be as honest as I could about what I knew and didn't, and how much I loved him and feared for his safety. I'd beg him to give himself a few more years, give me those years, before he fully became what Anna had said he would. Sitting across from me now, he sensed my fears; he always did.

"I'm going to be twelve, Mom," he said gently. "Twelve! I'm not a little kid anymore. I'm not your little boy."

"You'll always be my little boy."

"I can do things with . . . you know the changing . . . that I couldn't do before," he said, ignoring me. "I can take care of myself. I've done it on my own."

"When?" I challenged him.

"Plenty of times. I know how to kill it."

"No, you don't."

"You don't know anything," he sulked, and I had no reply to that because I didn't. Then the old Davey was back for an instant, the one who gave tender kisses and whispered to take a breath so I wouldn't worry. I reached for him, wanting to hug him like I always did, and he pulled away, self-conscious. I realized how much I would miss that child, how much I missed him already.

"We've got to help each other through this," I said, but he didn't answer. I wondered if he'd even heard me, and how long would it be before I lost him altogether?

When Cade rang the bell, Davey answered it.

"Hey, man, ready to head out?" he asked, throwing me a wide grin. I grinned back, wondering if he could see the worry that was in my eyes. I'd slipped on jeans and a pink tank and put on too much makeup, but I didn't care. If I could have painted a smile on my face, I would have done it, because there was nothing but sadness in my heart.

The minute we got in Cade's car, Davey stuffed his

iPod earbuds into his ears. He liked nu metal groups I'd never heard of, and when I asked him about them, he'd just shrug and grin. I glanced at him, then at Cade, intent upon driving.

Nobody talked much, which was good because my thoughts weren't in the car. They were with Anna and her bitter little smile, her hard little eyes. I remembered how it had been when Davey was six, and we ran for the first time. It was Connecticut then, us riding on the bus, bags full of McDonald's burgers and fries. I'd gotten money from the bank and bought a used Civic when we got to Willimantic, an old mill town that had seen better days. It was a red car that Davey loved, and we'd driven to Rhode Island, far enough away, a small state so nobody from Anna's funeral would know where we'd gone. It had been an adventure, me and Davey. He thought we would find someplace to settle, have our own house just the two of us, he used to say . . . and maybe a pet, he'd always add, even though he knew that couldn't happen.

A year later, folks in our building started complaining about a stray dog—wolf, somebody said—hanging around, prowling in from nowhere. I knew it had found us. It wouldn't go away, and it chased Davey to his bus one morning. We left quick after that. Davey had seen the eyes, and he knew it had come. That was it, Anna used to say, it could get your scent and find you, no matter where you ran.

I used to wonder if it was my imagination, seeing things that weren't there, being too scared to confront what might be, running from beasts I'd conjured up from Anna's stories, but then there'd be some telltale sign—the glance of a woman with one eye bright red, not quite closing; a dog's muzzle for lips; a wolf's ear sneaking out from inside a hat; or the fleeting sight of Anna, showing up and disappearing like she did, warning us from a place she couldn't return from.

"I don't have any pennies, but there's a quarter in change in my pocket. I'd say whatever's on your mind is worth at least that." Cade broke into my thoughts. "Whatever he's listening to must be pumping," he added with a nod at the backseat. "Typical tweener. Are you ready for what comes next?" He must have noticed my confused look and added, "Tweener. Between ten and thirteen. It's got its own title these days. I'd say he's typical."

Davey was anything but typical, and this dear man sitting so cheerfully beside me knew nothing about us, and that thought brought tears into my eyes and a lump into my throat. He knew the simple stuff—that Davey liked to read about magic, and I liked to sketch flowers. That Davey was getting into heavy metal, and that old-school pop—Aretha, Mary J—was my thing. That Davey loved navy blue—as close to black as he could get, and I loved any shade of lavender. Not a bit of it made a difference. By next week, we would disappear, and he would have had no idea who we really were or where we'd gone. I hadn't lied to him, but I was a liar. I swiped at a tear that slipped down my cheek.

"Hey, what's wrong?" Cade glanced at me, then at Davey to make sure he couldn't hear us. "Why are you crying?" I didn't answer; I couldn't. "Will you tell me later? Maybe tonight, after we drop Davey off at Luna's?

You want to come to my place? For some tea or something?"

"Something like a drink," I said, thinking more of myself than of him.

"No, for me." He focused on the road again, then spoke, as if choosing his words carefully. "I told you about that setback I had a couple of weeks ago. I don't think I told you what brought it on. A guy was killed downtown, the same way Dennie was, and it brought the whole thing back, not that I could forget it. Did Luna mention it?"

"About the drinking, but not about why it happened." I didn't want to dwell on what had happened to Mack.

"There's still that wild man dwelling inside, yearning to get out."

"Having a drink when you're down doesn't make you a wild man."

"No, what makes you a wild man is not facing up to stuff that still hurts you, burying my grief until it comes out wild and unruly."

"Maybe that's just another way to deal with fear and sorrow."

"Like running away?"

I didn't answer that; I didn't dare.

"But it's not like it was before, like I told you before." He snuck a look at me to see if I remembered, and I managed a smile, a small one, to let him know I did. "But the cops coming over like they did, asking questions, drove me right into that bottle of Jim Beam, and I finished it off. So much for the drink you wanted." He smiled at himself, making light of it. "Guess I should have waited till I was stone sober to call Luna, so she wouldn't tell all my business."

"She told me because she knew how much I care about you," I said, which made him smile.

"The thing of it is, anything can set me back, to where I was. I know that now, and that's scary as hell. I've told one of my secrets, I want to hear yours."

"So that's one of your secrets, that you drink when you get depressed?"

"Up until I met you, I was burying myself in a bottle almost every other night. Second secret: I can't handle it, and I've been known to pass out cold. Third: I'm scared I'll end up like my father. That's three. And I've got plenty more." He followed with one of his quick half smiles.

"Three for three, right?"

"There's a lot to tell." I stared at the road. A lot *not* to tell.

"One secret at a time, that's all I want. Drop Davey off at Luna's, and spend some time with me tonight. Okay? I'm going to hold you to it. We've known each other long enough to be honest, Raine. I know how I'm beginning to feel about you, how much I care about you. I've been through too much to do anything but play fair. I can't play games anymore with anyone."

The way he said it touched me because I knew I would have to tell him that we were leaving. But I couldn't tell him why. Not all of it. Never. Davey was still rocking to whatever he was listening to. I caught his eye and winked at him. He looked puzzled, then nodded as if telling me he was okay, too, that everything was going to be okay.

"Mom, what's that on your face?" he said from the backseat, louder than he should because of the earphones.

"Too loud," Cade said just as loudly, gesturing toward his ears.

"You got black streaks running down your face, Mom."

"No napkins this time." As I dug into my bag for a Kleenex, Cade's words and glance told me he remembered when he'd wiped the milk off my chin in the restaurant that first time we had coffee together.

"Were you crying?" Concern was in Davey's voice, and it hurt to hear it. I never wanted him to know I cried.

"No."

"What, then?"

"Allergies," I said.

Even Davey didn't believe that; he grimaced in disgust.

Cade threw me an amused look. "Raine, you are one of the most secretive women I've ever met. But I've always loved a mystery."

Not this one, I thought. You don't want to solve this one. Mack came into my mind again. Everywhere we went, it found us, after months, a year; this time it had been nearly three, but it knew. It had found Mack. He hadn't told it where we were, because he didn't know, and it had killed him. And Dennie? That made no sense at all, except she lived near Luna, and it must have known that, too.

About a week. That's how much time you've got, Raine, so if you're going to go, you best be gone by then.

We'd be long gone by then.

"You all ready to do this thing?" Cade's tone was carefree, but the confidence in his voice saddened me. He'd begun to believe there could be more to us—as a couple with a kid—than would ever be possible.

Run. Run. Run. That was all I knew and that was all I would ever know—get out of here and away from him and the me that had begun to feel again.

"Yeah," Davey said, as enthusiastic as Cade, as they both climbed out of the car.

"Excuse me, a lady should always have the car door opened for her," Cade apologized, then came to my door to open it. "One thing to remember, Davey, when you get to that point. Something my dad never taught me."

"Who taught you?"

"Me," Cade said as the three of us headed into the fair.

It was crowded, noisy, and filled with color. Red and white balloons bobbed in the air, and yellow streamers were strewn across the branches of trees. The air was filled with the smell of hot dogs grilling, popcorn popping, and funnel cakes frying. Booming music and exuberant laughter seemed to pour in from all corners of the playground. From somewhere a rap group screamed rhymes, a brass band played hit tunes from the '80s, and kids laughed and shouted like they'd lost their minds. The noise and merriment were contagious, and I was swept with a sense of optimism and excitement. It had rained two days before and the ground was still muddy, which seemed to add to the fun of kids who gleefully stamped around grounds filled with booths selling swirly cotton candy and cheap toys. The rides—a pint-sized Ferris wheel, rickety roller coaster, and mechanical swings—were all in need of paint, but nobody cared; lines circled the ticket booths.

"Hey, Mr. Richards, how you doing?" yelled a boy in an oversized T-shirt, hair shaved to his scalp. He was about the same age as Davey and was followed by two other kids, one with an earring in his left ear, the other with a Nets cap like Davey's. "Is this kid your son?" the boy with the earring asked, giving Davey the once-over.

"No, he's a student like you."

"She his mama?"

"Yep."

"Hey, kid, what school you go to?" asked the kid in the T-shirt. Stunned, Davey dropped his head.

"You guys here by yourselves?" Sensing Davey's discomfort, Cade shifted attention away from him.

"Nah, my dumb sister's here somewhere," said the boy with the Nets cap. "Hey, kid, you down with the Nets?"

"Yeah," Davey said, comfortable on familiar territory.

"Who you listening to?" The boy with the shaved head pointed to the iPod earphones hanging around Davey's neck.

"Nu metal. Papa Roach, Disturbed, Chimaira."

"Wow, cool."

I glanced at Cade, who rolled his eyes.

"Want to hang out?" he asked.

"Yeah, sure," Davey said, trying to be cool, but asking my permission with his eyes.

Cade mouthed he'll be fine, and gave me a nod that said he'd keep an eye on him.

"See you later," I said as casually as I could.

Papa Roach and the Nets had given Davey a path to normalcy, at least for an afternoon, and I sure wasn't going to take it away. The boys strolled toward a concession stand. Cade bought me a giant wad of yellow cotton candy as we followed discreetly behind them.

I caught a glimpse of myself in a long, distorted mirror in front of a fun house, and cringed at the black smudges on my face and cotton candy that had found its way into my hair. The women's restroom was in a field house close to the fairground, and after Cade promised he'd keep an eye on Davey, I ducked into it. The narrow room was lit by fluorescent bulbs that cast a greenish, surreal light on the checkered floor littered with paper towels and empty soda cans.

As I wiped black smudges off my cheek, a woman came in, ducking quickly into one of the stalls. It was her smell, floating in from somewhere I couldn't place, that caught my attention. Was it Anna's scent? It couldn't be, but I knew I'd smelled it before, after the funeral—pine touched with rosemary, smothered by a mix of wildflowers that only Anna knew how to blend.

Another woman came in then, pretty and plump, accompanied by a child with tightly braided cornrows.

"I hate it when mascara streaks on your face." She smiled, and I nodded in agreement. She had a quick friendly grin, and when she and the child left, I wanted to leave with them, but something made me linger. I needed to see who this person was who smelled so much like Anna.

When she came out, she took her place at the sink next to mine, avoiding my eyes. Despite the heat, she wore a soiled black raincoat buttoned to the top and covering what looked like a lace blouse. We faced each other in the cracked mirror, she applying powder two shades too light, me dabbing at my cheeks at stains no longer there. When she stopped to search through her pocketbook, I studied her face. Could it be *her* after all this time? Was I seeing someone who wasn't here?

Round eyes, as black and hard as onyx, stared back at me from a bronzed face as old and puckered as a spoiled apple. I scanned her face again, risked staring, then realized there was no resemblance to Anna: the hair was different, as gray as steel but trimmed.

But I could be mistaken, so many years had passed. There was a shimmer of recognition in her eyes, for just a moment, and then a smile, white teeth, sharp and pointed. A wolf's teeth. My heart began to pound. But then, just as quickly, she closed her lips, hiding what I'd seen.

"Doba? Is that you," I asked her anyway. She didn't move. "How did you find me? How did you know I was here?" I couldn't hide the panic in my voice, the trembling underneath.

"Leave me alone!" Her voice was low, almost a whimper, not at all like Anna's with its strong, mellow tone. But it had been years since Anna's funeral, I couldn't remember how Doba's voice had sounded. I had only seen her once, and written her from time to time. I had to be wrong. Fearful, the woman drew back from the sink. I realized she was as afraid of me as I'd been of her.

"Leave me alone," she said again, her eyes wide and frightened, not the hard ones I'd seen before. Had I reached the point where I was scaring strangers in a public restroom? I stepped back, not wanting to alarm her. She turned to the mirror, ignoring me now as she patted on more makeup, brushing blusher onto her cheeks until they were a bright garish red. She was a helpless old woman, homeless probably, not seeing reality as it was. My imagination had gotten the better of me.

"Ma'am, I'm sorry. I didn't mean to . . ."

Her smile was fleeting, bashful yet not quick enough to hide the teeth that poked from behind her lips. I hadn't imagined those. What had she done to herself? What craziness had made her file them sharp like that? I thought about my dying grandmother on my father's side, the things she had done to herself near the end—the dresses worn inside out, the hair combed with honey, fingernails filed to a point, like this one had done to her teeth. She'd lived with us only briefly, but I was a child and in her own way so was she. We'd connected as children, what was her name? I'd forgotten, because it was rarely said. Mamie? Melanie?

Poor, sad thing.

Like this one.

As I turned to go, I glimpsed, or thought I did, something on her finger—a twist of gold and silver encircling turquoise found and set for a beloved daughter. The woman jerked her hand below the sink, hiding it from my view. Yet it had been so long ago that I'd seen that ring, that her response could have been one of fear, an attempt to hide a precious gem from someone who frightened her, someone she thought might steal it.

There was chatter outside the door. Loud laughter, louder voices, as two women entered: one tall with short red hair; the other older with streaked gray hair in a short natural. Mother and daughter, I assumed, with their similar looks and easy camaraderie. The woman's eyes darted from me to the women. Was she scrutinizing them for strength? For weakness? Or was she simply curious? Had they made her remember a daughter lost or long gone? She shook her head as if shaking something out and sighed slowly as if puzzled. I left the room before the women could see me trembling.

The sun, blazing and hot, hit me as if forcing truth upon me as I fell against the building, angry at myself for being so suspicious and fearful, puzzled by my own response. Luna's words last night and Mack's death had left me unsure of myself, of reality.

Cade called on my cell phone, his voice relaxed and amused, to make sure he hadn't missed me, and to say that Davey was having a good time. He's fine, don't worry about him so much, he said. It's good for him to be around kids his own age. I detected a critical note in his tone. He'd hinted before that I was overly protective. How could I be anything else? Are you okay, Raine? he said. I could hear the concern in his voice. Fine, I assured him. There's always lines in ladies' rooms. What else could I say, that I'd scared a poor homeless woman because I thought she was somebody I'd seen years ago at a funeral?

The woman came out as I spoke to him, hobbling like she had when she came in, one heel higher than the other, and when she saw me, she stopped and stared, eyes filled with rancor, then disappeared into the crowd.

My cell phone rang again, and Luna's name flashed on the screen.

"You okay?" I could hear anxiety in her voice.

"Fine, how come you asked like that?"

"No reason."

"Yes, there is."

"Something in your voice. Tell me what happened." So I told her the truth about what I'd seen, my self-doubt and the way I'd frightened some poor, harmless woman.

"So who did you think she was?"

"Anna's cousin. Doba."

"Now, that's strange," Luna said, pausing between each word. "Right after you left, a woman rang my bell looking for you and Davey, said she'd come by because not many people have the last name Loving, and that was your name before you married. Said she was related to Davey, second cousin, and needed to tell you something."

"Did you tell her where we were?" My heart rolled in my chest, beating fast like it had when the woman shuffled into the restroom, like it had when the dog nibbled at my hand outside of Starbucks.

"No. But she did wait in the back for a while, said she'd spotted that swing from the street and hadn't swung in one since she was a girl, asked if she could sit in it for a spell. Struck me as a little odd, but I didn't see any harm in it, since she said she was kin to the boy. Said she just needed to get off her feet and admire my garden. I went back inside, and heard the swing creaking when she sat down."

"Did you let her in the house?"

"No, she went through the bushes in the back."

"How did she look?"

"Well-dressed. Fresh-pressed white suit. You know what she did have, though, was a ring like those earrings you have. Held it up so I could take a look at it. Didn't have a thumb, poor thing. Lost it in an accident, she said. You can't do much in life without a thumb. That's why I noticed the ring."

"Is she still there?"

"No. Sat in the swing a minute or two, then left."

"You get a sense of people, don't you?"

She paused before she spoke. Luna could be as secretive about her gift as Davey was about his. "Sometimes."

"What did you get from her?"

"It doesn't work like that, Raine. I've got to touch a person, stand close before I can tell. And there was a screen door and a foot of space between us. She didn't let me get that close. She just went around the back and sat on the back porch, like I said."

If it *was* Doba, she had seen Davey at Mack's that day, and in the church. But he was taller and stronger than he was then, and with a man and a bunch of kids she didn't know. Or maybe I had the whole thing wrong. Maybe she had sought me out to give a warning, to tell me that whatever was after us was getting closer. To let me know that I had to leave and find another place to hide. Maybe she knew how to kill it. At Anna's funeral there had been that uncle whose name nobody would speak. Was he the thing that stalked us?

Don't trust nobody. Not family. Not friend.

I pasted on a carefree smile when I joined Cade by the Ferris wheel and closed my eyes as it creaked upward into the sky. Evening was coming, and the fair was lit with red and yellow lights that sparkled everywhere. I spotted Davey at one of the games, throwing a ball through a hoop as his newfound posse, as Cade called them, cheered him on. When we reached the top, Cade kissed me sweet and tenderly, and I snuggled close, enjoying his body squeezed next to mine, the softness of his lips.

We stopped at a diner on the way home, a typical Jersey one filled with the smell and sounds of hamburgers being fried and simmering chili. "This place reminds me of Mack," Davey whispered in my ear when we went inside, and I knew that despite the fun of the day, nothing had changed.

Night still lay before us.

11

cade

Dennie was on Cade's mind as he drove them home. He'd never been much good at reading women. It was one of the things Dennie had teased him about, hinting that like most men, he thought with his "small head" rather than the big one on top of his neck. Just thinking about her voice when she said it, the funny way she would shake her head followed with a quick eye roll, made him smile. He glanced at Raine now, studying her tight lips, fingers folded neatly in her lap with their bright red nails matching the color of her lipstick. She was coiled so tightly, he wondered what would happen if he touched her, so he did, lightly on her elbow.

"You okay?"

"Fine," she said too quickly. She gazed out the window not with the casual demeanor of simply enjoying the ride but with a furtive uneasiness, as if searching for someone in the night. Davey, earphones in ears, gazed into the darkness, too, but there was a relaxed smile on his lips, as if reliving the day, and that quickened Cade's heart, made him glad they'd come.

Raine worried him. Each time they were together—and it had been nearly every day in the past few weeks—he felt closer to her. It scared him how quickly he'd grown to care about her. He was as wary as he'd been those first few weeks of loving Dennie, falling so quickly, deeply, that he couldn't catch his breath. Yet this was different, slower. The instant he met Dennie—in the cafeteria when he'd dropped his wallet and she had picked it up—she surprised him. It had shocked him—weird thing for a strange woman to do, he'd thought, until she smiled, and he, Mr. Badass, was caught in her grin.

Raine? He knew himself in love. This was close to it, but something had to change between them. He couldn't take another heartbreak, even a little one. He knew that, too.

"Did you have a good time?" He didn't think she heard him, she seemed so lost in thought. "Raine?"

She turned away from the window with a smile that wasn't quite one and nodded. "Better than I've had in a long time."

"Sure about that?"

"Yeah. I've got a lot of stuff on my mind, Cade. That's all."

"Davey seemed to have enjoyed himself."

Her smile was full-blown now, no doubt how she felt about that. "Thanks, Cade."

"For what?" He noticed her eyes were moist. Tears. Again.

"For everything. For being there for me, for my son."

"Hey. You know how . . . Yeah, okay, thanks." You know

152

how I feel about you, he'd almost said, but he'd told her that already, he realized. In the car, coming over, with that talk about not playing games. She hadn't said much then, hadn't fallen over herself assuring him that she felt the same way about him, that she had the same feelings. Maybe she didn't. But it had been bad timing to say anything with Davey sitting in the backseat.

That scared him, too, how close he'd gotten to Davey. Watching the boys talking and walking together, keeping an eye on them but not close enough to let them know, it was like being a father, the father he'd always dreamed of becoming, the one he'd never had. That was the best thing about today, seeing Davey in his own element, with friends. Like a normal kid.

"So are we still on for tonight?" For those secrets you promised to tell me, he almost said but didn't, for something else he was afraid to admit to himself. Was that a sigh he heard, coming from her so softly? Was it that hard for her to be alone with him? This would be one of the few times they were completely alone. Not in a movie theater, restaurant, or sitting on Luna's back stairs while he watched her draw. Alone with him in the house he used to share with Dennie. Maybe he wasn't ready for that yet either. Even to talk. Only to talk.

"Yeah," she said. "But I need to tuck Davey in first."

"Tuck Davey in?" He raised his eyebrow so high, Raine laughed—at the thought of it, he was sure. As if anyone could tuck in a fast-growing eleven-year-old boy who had just recently discovered hip-hop and heavy metal.

"You know what I mean," she said, and he nodded

like he did, but he didn't. She was far too protective of her son, who struck him as more than able to take care of himself. When he'd first met Davey, he wasn't sure exactly how old the boy was, somewhere between nine and ten, he'd guessed, but the boy had grown up both physically and emotionally in the past few months, as emotionally mature as any eleven-year-old going on fourteen could be.

Sometimes when he looked at Davey he saw himself at that age. The awkwardness and secretive longings. The sadness touched with bravado and vulnerability. Maybe that was why he liked teaching kids that age, trying to find that forgotten space between boyhood and adolescence that was within himself.

His father's drinking hadn't really gotten to him until then. He'd always been aware of it, but it wasn't until he was eleven that he'd understood all the shit that came with it, what the word "drunk" really meant, even though he'd heard his mother hurl it at his old man a hundred times a day, out loud and under her breath, until the night she died.

Lousy drunk, useless drunk, lazy drunk, disgusting drunk, filthy drunk.

Maybe someday he'd be able to talk about his mother to Raine. He'd been married to Dennie a year before he could bring himself to share the depth of the wound his mother's death had left. Davey talking about his "weirdness" had brought out memories of his own. He thought again about the boy at the street carnival today, and how after his initial discomfort when Ken had asked about his school, how quickly he'd fit in.

He'd ask her about the school again tonight, he decided. It was near the end of August, and she should have made some kind of decision by now. He glanced over at her again, her eyes focused so intently on the darkness, hands rigidly folded in her lap. Why hadn't she bothered to tell him how she felt about him? Hadn't he made it clear how important she was, they both were, to him?

"Maybe an hour or so, about eight? Will your baby be tucked in by then?" He grinned to let her know he was teasing, and she smiled back briefly, her face turning serious again.

"Maybe a little later. Something has . . . well, come up, and I need to talk about it with him tonight."

"Something serious?"

"Yeah."

Short and sweet and soft, the yeah. If he hadn't been listening closely, he wouldn't have heard it.

❧

He hadn't realized what a mess his place was until he saw it as he imagined Raine would. Dirty dishes piled high in the sink, dust clumped on the floor in tiny balls, grimy spots on the kitchen floor. Davey was used to it; Raine wouldn't be. They stopped having tea here after their first date. He swept under furniture and soaked the dishes in the sink. After pulling out the vacuum cleaner, which hadn't been used since Dennie's death, he tried to turn it on, then realized he had no idea where the switch was. He found it tucked under a lever, cursed to himself about the craziness of putting it there, and made a swipe

at the floors and the rug in the living room. When he finished, he realized with some disgust that it looked pretty
much the same.

The woman is coming for . . . whatever, he reminded
himself, but he knew it was more than that. Slowly, me-
thodically, he began to clean all the places he thought she
might go. He took the grimy glasses off the living room
coffee table, slippers from under the couch, moved papers
he had yet to file.

He glanced at Dennie's office. The door was tightly
closed. He checked it to make sure.

He thought about cleaning upstairs—the bedroom,
bathroom—and then felt foolish that he would even
consider taking Raine upstairs, then spent the next ten
minutes guiltily wondering what it would be like to
make love to her. He'd certainly thought about that
more than once. Then, out of nowhere, he began to
wonder why exactly he'd invited her over in the first
place.

"To talk," he'd told her, realizing how insistent he'd
been about sharing whatever was on her mind. He'd asked
for some kind of truth-telling—sharing of truths, he'd
called it. But maybe it was none of his business. Maybe
she didn't want the relationship to go any further; women
were the ones to lead in this kind of thing, not men. He'd
never been good at doing it, anyway.

He thought about taking a shower, then remembered
he'd taken one that morning. He thought about dashing
to the store to get something to serve—cookies, sandwiches, appetizers—then laughed out loud for his silly
anticipation. He could almost hear Dennie laughing at

him, too, then stopped to yell at himself about Dennie when he was considering being with another woman.

And what kind of a place was this to bring Raine, anyway, the house where your wife was murdered? But hadn't she been here before with Davey?

Should he call it off, ask her to meet him somewhere else, anywhere else, but it was nearly nine and there was nowhere else for them to go. Just to talk. And wasn't that what they were going to do?

We've known each other long enough to be honest. I know how I'm beginning to feel about you, how much I care about you. I've been through too much to do anything but play fair. I can't play games anymore with anyone.

He'd blurted out the words before he knew he was saying them, but it was the damn truth, that he was tired of the life he had and the way he was living it, and for the first time since Dennie's death, he had begun to see a light, and that light was Raine. She was here, and he had to know where they stood.

"Hard time getting Davey tucked in?" he joked when she stepped into the kitchen. She'd come in through the back door, like Davey always did. Hell, nobody came to the front door except the damn cops. The moment after the words left his mouth, he wished he hadn't said them. He couldn't ignore the wrinkles of distress on her forehead. "Come on in," he quickly added. Something about Davey, no doubt. Preteen shit. She'd tell him later if she wanted him to know.

They settled down at the kitchen table like they had when they were first getting to know each other, but there was uneasy distance between them now, and again he had second thoughts about having invited her. What did he have to say that hadn't been said already? Yet as he watched her sipping her Coke, so thoughtfully, oddly seductive, he was glad he had. After a few moments, he came out with what was really on his mind.

"I'm worried about you, Raine. I'm scared that I'm going to lose you; that you're going to disappear from my life the way you came into it, without a trace, and I don't think I could take that."

The look she gave him, so tender and deep, told him he had said the right thing, and as he had done before he took her hand, thinking how small and soft it was, how vulnerable. He saw tears come into her eyes. "What's going on, Raine? Every time I look at you, you're crying. Can't you tell me?"

"I don't know if I'm ready."

He decided to leave it there, not force anything else, and after a while, she laughed—a light, charming, devil-may-care chuckle that he knew was meant to put him at ease and suddenly he was.

"Want something to eat?"

"What do you have?"

He realized then what a stupid thing it was to ask, since he didn't have a damn thing, so he shrugged. He should have bought something, he realized, dips, chips. Dennie would scold him; he could almost hear her voice. You don't invite a lady on a date at your home and have nothing to serve her! What kind of suitor are you? Suitor!

A word only Dennie would use, and that thought made him smile.

"How about some popcorn?" He suddenly remembered the bag he'd bought for his class at the end of the year that he forgot to take to school.

"Sounds good. Do you have butter and salt?"

"That I do have." He went to the cupboard, pulled out the ancient bag of popcorn, and gave it to Raine. "Okay?"

"I think we need a pot with a cover, popcorn popper, microwave?"

"Oh—oh yeah, of course." Embarrassed that she'd had to ask, he quickly pulled out the cast-iron pot Dennie had used to pop corn and handed it to her.

"Cade, would you like me to pop it?" she asked with a patient, good-natured grin.

"Oh, no, no, of course not! Sorry," he muttered. Dennie always popped the corn when they made it. When he popped it now, it was always the microwave popcorn; he had no idea how to do it from scratch. He took back the pot, poured in some oil, the popcorn, placed it on a front burner, and began to shake. When smoke and the stench of scorched popcorn filled the small kitchen, he realized too late he'd put in too much corn and not enough oil.

"Damn it!" he mumbled, snatching the pan off the burner and throwing the whole mess—pot, burned popcorn, smoking oil—into the sink. "Can't even do that right."

Raine, standing behind him, watched as he dumped the contents into the garbage disposal. "Hey, you do just about everything else right," she said. Without warning, she kissed him on the back of his neck. It was an awkward, tender kiss, sweetly given, which he felt straight down to his groin.

"Should burn popcorn more often if that's what it gets me." He realized after the words left his mouth how phony they sounded, like something out of a silly romantic comedy. But she kissed him again, turning his head around to touch his lips with her full, soft ones and his body, the pleasure of her against him warming him everywhere he felt her. He pulled away, self-conscious about his reaction, not sure if he wanted her to know what his body was telling him to do.

That was the problem with being a man, he thought, you couldn't hide what your intentions were; your dick always gave you away. As a kid, slow-dancing with a neighborhood girl for the first time, he had gotten so hard so quick, he'd been embarrassed to pull away, knowing it would be standing out like a flagpole, straight and proud, in front of him. Luckily, the room had been dark, lights turned out, moonlight seeping in from the half-pulled blinds the only illumination. He'd been proud of it, though, how hard it got, but ashamed of it, too, because it telegraphed to Linda, Marsha, whatever her name had been, that he was her slave. You want to do it, don't you? she'd whispered, hot and wet into his ear, as she licked his earlobe with the lusty inexperience of a fourteen-year-old. You know where to put it? she'd asked, mocking him, and he'd nodded. So they'd gone into a dark corner of the basement and done "it" on the floor. He'd fucked, had sex, made love with so many women since then, he had a hard time attaching names to faces, and only the special ones stood out, the ones who took his heart and twisted it to the point where he didn't know it belonged to him.

With Dennie, he'd been nervous as hell that first time. Just watching her walk across the room—her round behind rhythmically bouncing to music only he could hear—was enough to send his dick throbbing in his trousers. She would study him, half-amused, like she did the research she always seemed to be reading—interested, curious, analytical—which used to drive him crazy. She had no idea how sexy she was.

Neither did Raine. The way she shrugged when puzzled or threw her head back and laughed whenever she did get it, all sparkling good humor. He loved to watch her talk to Davey, her tenderness and worry touched him in a place that his own mother had touched once, brought her gentle presence back to him. Yet at the same time he felt protective of her, so different from Dennie, who never seemed to need his protection. His passion for Raine wasn't the red-hot, throw-all-caution-to-the-wind lust he'd felt for his wife. He'd been there once and couldn't let himself go back there again, but this was a different heat, one that snuck up on him, then moved quickly to take over everything else: like good sense. Like vigilance.

Not wanting to risk looking at her, he scrubbed out the pot, read the directions on the back of the plastic popcorn bag, and carefully measured the oil and popcorn into the pot. When it was popped, he avoided the oversized red china bowl that Dennie used and poured popcorn with hot butter into a metal mixing bowl.

"Here you go. Better than the movies," he said, sitting

down across from her, delighted when she picked up a handful of popcorn and tossed it into her mouth like a kid would.

As they sat munching popcorn, avoiding each other's eyes, Cade wondered if she felt the same way he did, as wary of her feelings toward him as he was to her. The bright fluorescent lights of the kitchen bathed the room in garish light, and he wished they'd started out in the living room with its dim ceiling lights, soft cushiony couch, and big-screen TV. But when Raine gazed at him, the sorrow in her eyes was startling as it pulled at his heart, and he realized that this was the best place for them to be. Before they could relax, they needed to talk about the things that were bothering him, with no comfort to distract them.

"Why were you crying in the car today, Raine? What's going on, what's bothering you?" She sighed, so deeply and with such melancholy, he instantly wished he hadn't asked, but it was too late to take it back.

"We need to move again, Cade," she said without looking at him, and when she did, her eyes were so distant, he wondered if she was lying. "Something . . . well . . . we're leaving in a couple of days. It's been nagging—"

"What do you mean you're leaving? Just like that? You're going where?" He hadn't meant to raise his voice but he had, and her glance made him ashamed that he had done it. But he couldn't hide it; he didn't want to.

She stared at him as if she couldn't quite find the words to tell him more.

"You can't just leave like that, you can't just take Davey, make him pull up roots and—"

Her gaze grew tight and hard on his face. "We don't

have any roots, Cade. We never did. We weren't meant to stay here, and now we need to leave." Her voice was reasoned and calm, cold. He looked down at the kitchen table, at the nearly empty bowl of popcorn; everywhere but into her eyes.

"Why?" He realized too late that he sounded like a whiny kid.

"We just have to."

"That's not good enough."

"I know," she said in a small, anguished voice.

"Davey's going, too?" The minute after he asked it, he realized what a foolish question it was.

She answered with a slight smile, not really a smile at all, filled with as much sorrow as was in her eyes. "I just spent the last two hours arguing with him. But he knows what's up."

"And what exactly is that, Raine. What exactly is up?" His tone was harsh, angry, and he meant it to be, because suddenly he was mad and disappointed and wanted her to know it, to feel as hurt and empty as her words had made him feel. A dull sorrow followed by a pang of desperation filled him and a fear of loneliness settled just beneath his heart. Did he even have a right to feel it? He suddenly didn't give a damn one way or the other. "I guess I owe you an apology, don't I." Sarcasm rode each word. She glanced at him, wary and puzzled. "It's just like all this time, I thought maybe I meant something to you, that maybe you were feeling what I was, that maybe—well, it's all bullshit now, I guess, isn't it?" He grabbed the bowl of popcorn and threw what was left into the sink, and suddenly he didn't want to be around her. Anywhere but in this room.

"Cade, I—"

"There's nothing you can say, Raine. To come in here like this, after the fun we had today, after the things we've done . . . Well, I guess truth be told, we didn't do all that much, did we? Like, I said, I was so desperate for someone in my life, I guess I just imagined you were her, that you'd stick around."

"Please don't—"

"Well, you know it's like they say: People always tell you who they are if you listen, and you sure told me, didn't you? You were headed out of town the first time I met you, and you told me that." He felt like throwing things, like cursing her out, then himself for his feeling, but he just stood in front of the sink, avoiding her eyes, staring at the top of the garbage disposal, feeling like a fool. "Maybe you should just go," he said finally. "So I can get back to my life." And even as he said it, the dreariness of what his life had become came back to him: Jim Beam sitting in the cabinet; imaginary talks with his dead wife; the funk he'd been in since she died.

"Everything you felt was real, Cade. It was for me, too. I haven't been as happy since Elan died. I thought I'd never be that happy again." Raine's voice was so tiny, so thin, he could barely hear her. He looked at her now and away from the sink.

"Then why?"

"Remember what I told you about living in the present?" she said after a minute. "About how sometimes that's all I have, and you said you understood. Can't we just do that for tonight, Cade? Have that between us. Please. Please Cade, please."

His heart flinched at the pleading of her voice, the anguish in her eyes, and he went to her, and pulled her body into his. Almost like a sigh, he felt her give herself to him, as if handing him her life, and he knew that this was all she was able to give him—now—maybe forever. So he kissed her forehead, then her lips, and led her upstairs.

12

raine

It was easy to make love to him. I had slept with only one man before I met Elan and no one since he'd died. It was years since a man had touched me, thought of me like Cade did this night. Yet when I kissed him in the kitchen, it was for comfort rather than passion. I was grateful to him for being there, for rescuing me from Davey's raging anger. My inexperience half blinded me to what a kiss could do, how quickly it aroused. I'd been running as much from my son as toward Cade, and my kiss, as tender and gentle as it was, had been simply that. I didn't know where it would lead except suddenly I wanted him, and everything I'd forgotten about sex— the madness that blocked reason and second thoughts— came over me. The decision was made the moment I'd entered his house, the first time he'd kissed me good night, and the fleeting touch of his lips brought back the thrill I'd felt on the Ferris wheel earlier that evening.

I hadn't thought we would make love that night, hadn't planned on it—for as many times as I'd fantasized about him, imagined him stroking the intimate places in my body, imagined how his lips would feel on those parts of me that I'd never revealed before. I was breathless when he led me upstairs, and I thought about Davey and him always telling me to take a breath, but it wasn't that kind of breathlessness, and Cade was as breathless as I was.

We paused at the door of his bedroom. I was shy about entering a room he'd once shared with his wife, and he must have felt that way, too, but it was just for an instant. It was a pretty room, decorated with the same hand that had chosen the colors in the kitchen—but darker here, more sensual—deep rose instead of pink, white lace coverlet on the bed, sheer curtains that drifted to the floor in a graceful heap. A woman's room, but shared with a man she loved, that was clear to me the moment we entered. There were traces of her everywhere. The books—on every counter, surface—in neat piles on the large pink and gray Oriental rug that took up most of the floor, lying where'd she'd left them, untouched.

It was hard to imagine the kind of woman Dennie had been. He had described her in so many ways—whimsical one moment, practical the next. Smart yet gullible—and above all, honest—heart always perched on her sleeve. Cade, sensing my hesitation, took my hand, leading me into what I knew was his private, sacred place. It was clear he hadn't planned that we might make love. He was as wary as I was.

"Cade," I asked after a minute, "are you sure you want me to be here?"

"Of course," he said, his glance puzzled.

"Have you made love to anyone since she died?"

He sighed and dropped his eyes, embarrassed. "That obvious? I—well, I had a couple of chances but— Can we change the subject?"

"No. I need to know if this is what you really want to do. You're still so in love with Dennie, I wonder—"

"My wife is dead, Raine." He looked at me straight now, no shyness or hesitation. "I loved her so much, I thought I wanted to die, too, but that's changed since I met you."

"Are you sure you want to—?"

He pulled me to him and kissed me more passionately than he ever had before, answering the question in the only way it could be answered. "Okay?" he said, and I nodded that it was.

Despite the neatness of the room, *his* things were tossed about in messy abandon—socks on the floor, pants hung over chairs, shoes and mismatched sneakers by the side of the bed.

"Sorry for the mess," he said as he picked up socks, surveyed the room, then dropped them back where they'd been. "The sheets are clean," he added, a sheepish half grin on his face that made me laugh, and he joined me, both of us amused at ourselves, and what we were about to do. I sat down beside him on the bed, neatly made, surprisingly, and took his hand in mine, hoping to reassure him that nothing mattered but what I was feeling, what we both were. We kissed again, the charge that pulsed between us telling both of us where we were going and that it would be good.

"I loved Dennie, but she's gone, Raine. I want you in my life now. You and Davey. Do you understand that?"

I said nothing because there was no answer to his question.

He undressed quickly, first slipping a chain with a gold ring from around his neck and placing it in the bureau next to the bed. Seeing him naked before me—his arms and chest so taut and firm, his thighs thick with muscles, strong yet not distorted—told me how safe I would be with him, and everything I'd felt from the first moment I saw him came back to me in an instant, increasing my desire. He took my clothes off slowly, slipping off each bit of clothing, touching that part of my body it had covered, caressing, kissing me until I was completely undressed. And then, turning to me, slowly taking me into his arms, he pulled me into bed beside him.

There had always been a fervor, hidden though it was, in our kisses, touches, and now that we permitted ourselves the freedom to caress and explore each of those parts we'd only imagined, we exploded in a frenzy of desire.

I had not made love to a man since Elan. I was not sure how I would feel and respond to his touch, if I even had it in me after all these years to feel anything but reluctance, to give myself to another man so completely—but I did tonight to Cade. He entered my body slowly, as if seeking permission, which I quickly and eagerly gave, lunging into him with everything that was part of me, letting him know that I wanted to feel him inside me—to touch every part of me—as much as he wanted to be there.

There was a timelessness to our lovemaking, as if neither of us had been here before, but at the same time there was familiarity, as well, with him, his body, his touch. I was as at ease in his lovely, messy bed that smelled of the aftershave lotion he wore, and which I knew would send me into a spasm of desire next time I smelled it. We found comfort together in bed, delight, as much as I had sitting in the kitchen or that first time over his poorly made coffee, in the café, on our walks.

Freedom marked our lovemaking the second time. I had never been shy in bed with Elan, allowed him liberties I couldn't imagine giving another man, but things came so easily with Cade, there was no reluctance. It was as if everything had been saved from all those furtive touches, cautious kisses, unspoken desires and come forth in an intense rush of pleasure.

When we were finished, settled into each other's arms, I closed my eyes, pretending that we were just two normal people having made love for the first time, and discovering each other in ways that I'd never imagined. He kissed me once, twice on the forehead, and then on the lips, and I settled into his body, feeling him against me as I'd imagined I would all those times alone in my bed, but I knew this would be the one and only time this would happen between us. My eyes filled with tears as I looked away, not wanting him to see them. He turned my face toward him, softly kissing the tears that had fallen down my cheeks and onto my breasts.

"So you cry when you make love?" he asked, only half-joking.

"Sometimes."

"And this time you do, or is something else bothering you? Please tell me Raine. This . . . has meant . . ." He didn't finish, and I noticed his eyes had filled with tears, too. Embarrassed, he got up and turned his face from mine, trying hard to hide them. "Do you want something to drink? I have . . . whatever you want."

"Just you," I said. "Just you to stay with me awhile longer." He chuckled, giving one of his half smiles that I knew I was falling in love with, and pulled me close to him, his body telling me he was ready to make love again. And we did, drunk again with each other.

"Tell me why you cry so often," he said when we were finished and resting. His voice was the same one I knew he used to coax secrets from the kids he taught. "All you have to do is tell me what it is, and we can solve it together."

My sigh was weary and filled with anxiety because I knew he could never understand.

"Is it another man? I know you said there was no one, but—"

"No, Cade. There's nobody else."

"Is someone threatening you? You owe somebody money? I've got a little saved, not much, but whatever I have is yours." He chuckled slightly at that, but I knew he was telling the truth, and that anything he had he would give me as willingly and generously as he had shared his body. "Then what, Raine. Something with Davey? Is something going on with him?"

I've never been a good liar even though I've had a lot of practice. Running away and lying, that's been my life for the past few years. Running to and then from and then back to Anna with all her protective madness. Lying about who I was to half the people I knew who had grown to love me. Running before they could find out the truth. Lying to Mack and even to Davey about settling down somewhere and staying put, about finding a place where we could be happy and safe. Then running away, again and again and again. Lying to myself. Running from myself and what my child was, who he was.

Sometimes you reached a point where you just couldn't tell another lie without it rotting everything that's in you, and I knew resting next to Cade, after making love as ardently, passionately as we had and then peering into his eyes shadowed by grief yet deepened by his desire for me, that I was at that point.

"Tell me?" he said gently but firmly. I didn't say anything for a while, moved closer to him under the sheets, kissed the space under his chin, running my tongue down his chest, wondering if maybe I could put it off if we made love again, but he pulled away this time, not cruelly but thoughtfully, as if he'd made up his mind and this was what he'd decided. I edged away from him and sat up, pulling the cover over my breasts. He grabbed my hand and kissed my fingertips and then pulled me toward him, gently kissing my lips again.

"Now," he said with a determination that made me smile despite what I was feeling.

"You asked for it," I said, half joking, but only half.

"Nothing can be that bad," he said with a teasing,

coaxing smile, and that made me smile, too, because I remembered what Luna had told me all those days ago, how the telling was worse than the told half the time, and maybe she was right. So I leaned back against the pillows on the bed and started to tell it, but I couldn't look him in the eyes. I didn't want to see what might come into them.

"You remember the first time you met me and Davey, in the church that time with Luna?"

"Yeah, of course."

"Then you remember how scared Davey was, how I couldn't find him for a minute, how he disappeared?"

He was puzzled and I realized he'd left before I discovered Davey was gone. He'd gone to get his car. "What I do remember was when we got over to Luna's, he seemed scared. You said he got scared sometimes. What did you mean by that?" He studied me, determined now to get any truth I was hiding. I was tired of hiding now; he could have it all.

"Something was chasing him."

"What?"

"Something that wanted him dead, and Davey ran from it."

"What do you mean wanted him dead?"

"Something that's been chasing us a long time, Cade. Something that won't give up until it gets him, me."

"Who are you talking about? What do you mean by it?"

"I don't know," I said quietly, ignoring his eyes wary with disbelief.

"Raine, how could you not know who wants to kill you and your son?"

"Because it or he or she is not human, and it changes each time it finds us."

He pulled back from me in disbelief, his breath sticking in the back of his throat. He studied my face, not sure what to say, and that look made me wish I'd said nothing, let our time together with all its sweetness and longing be only the "now" we'd said it would be. But it was too late. His eyes were wide with questions, I went on.

"Do you remember that time, that first time in the Starbucks when you told me that what murdered Dennie was inhuman and—" Cade started to interrupt me, but I put my fingers on his lips, like I used to do with Davey when I wanted him to be quiet and listen, and he did, reluctantly, letting me finish. "Remember you told me that it was like some animal killed her, like it killed Mack."

"Walter Mack?" he looked puzzled, and I realized I'd never told him about Mack, about me and Davey and Mack. "You knew him?"

"I used to work for him. The thing that butchered him was looking for me, Cade, for me and Davey."

He pulled away from me then, standing up to walk across the room. He picked up his boxer shorts, taken off and thrown there in our rush to make love. Slipping them on as if he felt vulnerable, as if he wasn't quite sure he could reveal every part of himself to me, but he came back to bed, sat on the edge, and I breathed a sigh of relief; he wasn't leaving. I knew what his next question would be.

"And Dennie?"

"Maybe it was a mistake or maybe it knew I would end up staying with Luna. . . ." But even as I said it, I knew that didn't make any sense. His head collapsed into his hands, covering his eyes so I couldn't see what was in them.

"Or it was after her because of the stuff she was studying," he said, his voice muffled so low, I could hardly hear him.

"What was she studying, Cade?" Maybe I was wrong, maybe it hadn't been looking for us after all.

"I thought I told you, I thought maybe Luna . . . Myths. Navajo myths. Skin-walkers. Shape-shifters. Shit that doesn't make any sense, that doesn't exist. Maybe she stumbled onto something, got involved with some crazy man. I can't talk about it anymore, Raine. Please—"

"We have to talk about it," I said, and he turned to me, and then away. "Because there's more."

"More?"

"It's why I'm leaving. It found us."

He tilted his head as if he hadn't quite heard me, didn't know if he could believe me, as if maybe I were imagining things. "Found you? What do you mean, found you?"

"Found us, Cade. It always finds us because it needs to."

"This doesn't make sense, Raine. How do you know? Because of the guy who died? Because . . . Look, you can't leave because of some random murder—even Dennie was probably something else, not connected. How do you know that, Raine?" He grabbed my shoulders to make me face him and look into his eyes, which I didn't want to do. "Raine!" He pulled me to him again, and I let him do it, enjoying the strength of his pull as he drew me next to him.

"I know because I always do."

He let me go then, and I edged away from him, back to my side of the bed even though I wanted to be close to him again, to have him hold me like he had before, to pretend that this could be the beginning not the end between us.

"Is it just a matter of protecting you and Davey? You must know how I feel about the two of you by now. That I'll do anything—" He stopped then, and I wondered if he was thinking about Dennie and what had happened to her, about Mack. And then I realized that maybe he didn't believe me at all, not completely, anyway. How could he? "What aren't you telling me?" he said, looking into my eyes, trying to see what was there, and as I gazed into his, I could see a flicker of suspicion, a trace of doubt.

"It's about Davey," I said.

"Are you afraid that we won't be able to protect him from . . . whatever you think is threatening him. Is that it? Raine, I'm on your side. I don't want to let you go. I can't let you go, don't you understand that by now?" The rush of his words and the anguish in his voice shot through me, and I felt a pang deep within my heart.

"I need to tell you about Davey," I said more softly than I meant to, and he bent toward me as if he hadn't heard me.

"Davey?"

I nodded, took a breath, not quite sure where to begin so I reminded him that he'd asked me once if Davey was afraid he'd inherited an illness from his father, and I started there, back to our first date. He smiled, and I knew he was remembering like I did; the memory made me smile, too, but it was a bittersweet one, more bitter than sweet.

"You said, in a way he had . . . inherited something," he said. I was surprised how closely he remembered what I'd told him.

"But it was a half answer, not the whole thing—"

"Raine, if—"

"No. Listen to me! Don't say anything until I finish." My raised voice surprised him, but he nodded, acknowledging that he would hear what I had to say.

"Davey can change shapes," I said. "He's what some people call a shape-shifter or werewolf, and when they're at their worst, they are called skin-walkers—that's what Anna called them, in some language I couldn't understand. It happens when he gets scared or angry or sad. It happens to others with the shape of the moon." He opened his mouth to talk; I touched his lips with my fingers. I had to get it all out now, not go back to it later. Make it done and over now, and he would know once and for all what my truth—what Davey's truth—was and had been.

"His grandmother Anna had it, this gift he has, that's

what she called it anyway, and his father, Elan, must have had it, too. It's been small animals up to now—rabbits, squirrels, mice, but as he gets older, it will change. He will grow meaner, fiercer."

Cade leaned toward me, staring at me as if I'd lost my mind, then drew away, saying nothing, staring at the bed, at the space between us.

"Davey is one of those things that tore apart your wife, Cade, can you understand that? He has that rage within him, and, I'm scared it will take him over. My son is the youngest of his pack, Anna said, and when he grows into his strength, he will lead it. The thing that is chasing us wants to kill him before he can grow into a man. Before he can defeat it, so there's nothing I can do now except run."

He touched the side of my face, my lips with his fingertips as I'd touched his before, as if trying to silence me, as if he thought I'd suddenly gone mad, sitting here on the bed, telling what must have sounded like some crazy woman's tale. "Raine, are you—?"

"Do you think I would make something like this up? How could you think that I could do that?" Tears filled my eyes and then his as he pulled away from me, back to his side of the bed.

"Listen to me with your heart if not with your head, and you will know I'm telling the truth because we both know what happened to Dennie. It was looking for Davey."

Cade turned away then, his face distorted with anguish.

We couldn't face each other; I was as closed off from

him as he was from me. I had told him the truth, what he wanted and needed to know, and I knew he believed me. It was time for me to leave, to go back to Luna's, to pick up my son and finish packing, for us to be on our way.

I sat on the edge of the bed for a while, not quite ready to leave, as I remembered the beginning of our evening. His teasing words about my "tucking Davey in," the sweetness of our kisses downstairs, even the burning of popcorn, and it seemed as if it had happened long ago. Nothing was the same now.

I thought about Davey then, and what he'd said before I came over here. I remembered the rage in his voice as he'd screamed at me before I left his room.

❧

"I'm not going. No matter what you think or want, I'm not going. Just like I told you before."

"We'll talk about it later," I'd told him. "Luna will be out for a while. She's going to visit a friend, but she'll be back. . . . Did you hear me?" His head was tilted like it was when he heard Anna's words and danced to her silent tunes.

"What are you thinking, Davey?"

"I'm not thinking, I'm feeling."

"What are you feeling?"

"Something you can't understand."

"Are you shifting?"

"It doesn't matter, does it?"

"Please tell me, Davey. Don't cut me out."

He didn't say anything, then turned to me with more

sorrow than I could ever remember seeing in his eyes. "I don't have any choice," he said.

I'd thought about Cade then, that I should call him, tell him to forget it, just stay and sit awhile longer with Davey, but I needed to say good-bye to him, in my own secretive way.

"I love you, Davey," I said, and kissed him on the top of his head, and he gave me his special smile, the one that always broke on his face when I needed to see it most, and I'd left him staring into the darkness of his room.

What dreams do you have for him? Cade had asked me once—so long ago, it seemed. I knew the answer now: none.

✧

"Raine." Cade brought me back to him.

"It's time for me to go."

"Please stay with me awhile longer. Just for a time. Wherever you're going, whatever you're thinking, we're safe now, just for tonight."

And so I stayed, nestling close to him, believing he was right.

13

cade

Two hours before dawn, Cade awoke and thought he heard a dog growl, then realized it was nothing but the wind, so he closed his eyes and listened to the sound of Raine breathing easy and soft beside him. He kissed her shoulder as lightly as he could, and she smiled in her sleep. He drifted off himself, trying to recapture the remnant of a dream.

It was about Dennie, as his dreams often were, and he was happy as he always was when he saw her. She was sitting at her desk, dressed in the torn jeans and red cowl sweater she wore around the house, horn-rimmed glasses perched precariously on top of her head, fuzzy pink slippers loose and comfortable on her feet. He looked around her office, afraid of what he would find, fearful of something he wouldn't see but suspected was there, and then, still afraid, glanced at her again, and she grinned, saying it would be okay. She was talking into her recorder, pausing, stopping, listening, then abruptly turned it off. I'm fine and you will be, too, she said to him, although her lips were closed because she was smiling. Dennie! he screamed in his sleep, and she disappeared as she always did when he called her name.

He woke up, reaching for Raine like he used to for Dennie, but her side of the bed—pillow and sheet—were cold. Had she simply left the room, gone to the bathroom? But the air itself felt empty, devoid of breath and scent, and he knew he was alone.

He wondered for a second if he'd dreamed the whole thing: laughing in the kitchen, the comfort and warmth of her body when she yielded it to him, pushing his way inside her, and most of all, what she'd told him before they fell asleep—about what had killed Dennie, about Davey. Damn her! He got out of bed and pulled up the shades, letting sunshine brighten the room. Spotting a note on the bureau, he picked it up and read it quickly.

Cade,

Forgive me if I've caused you pain. I will cherish you forever and never forget this precious night, the last one we will ever spend together. Try to understand what I told you and why we need to leave as soon as we can. I am afraid of what will happen. Please allow me this space.

My love forever, Raine.

"Fuck!" he said, balling up the note and tossing it into the trash can at the side of the bureau. "Just fuck it!" Then feeling strangely contrite, he pulled it out of the trash and read it again. He sat down on the side of the bed to clear his head, to try to forget how he'd felt last night, the tenderness with which they'd made love, but her scent, the smell of the lemon lotion, oil, or whatever the hell it was she wore, lingered in the room, the bed, his skin, it seemed, and he wondered if he were imagining that, too—if one could imagine smells like you could sounds, like he'd imagined the dog howling before dawn.

What had she said about Davey, about him being one of those things that tore Dennie apart, about the rage he had within him? And for an instant, but not more than that, he'd felt rage boil within him toward the boy, sitting on his couch, playing chess, listening to him teach; Davey was a part of what had destroyed his life! He stopped himself then. She must be out of her mind.

He didn't give a damn what she said, Davey couldn't be what she thought he was. He knew enough about kids to see that. And that was key, wasn't it? What she *said* her son had within him. For the last ten years, he'd worked with kids—smart, dumb, crazy—and knew more than a bit about troubled ones. Hell, he'd been a troubled one himself. Davey wasn't troubled; he'd been with the kid a couple of hours, two or three times a week, and never saw any hint of that. Sad, sometimes scared, like the time he'd heard that dog. That had sure scared him, like it had scared her at Starbucks that day. Had the dog actually nipped her hand? Had it drawn blood?

Please allow me this space.

He could hear the pleading in her voice even though the words were written, and he knew he had no choice but to give her what she asked. But didn't he have rights, too? When someone touched your life, changed it as she had his, they owed you something even if they didn't know it. *He* knew it and had a right to find any truth he could. That was the only way you could heal, and he would sure need healing after this.

He showered, pulled on sweats, and went to the kitchen to make coffee, poured himself a cup, and spotted the remnants of the burned popcorn still in the sink. Funny how scorched popcorn made him recall the softness of her lips, and a shock of desire rammed itself through him despite his determination to keep her out of his mind. Then he thought about Davey and got angry all over again. What craziness was that, to make her say stuff like that about her own kid? She must be crazy as hell! Then suddenly from somewhere came Dennie's voice, and he stopped mid-sip, recalling a conversation they'd had so long ago:

It's all witchcraft, as far as I'm concerned. And I don't believe in witches.

You would if you read the stuff I've read.

What had she read? What had she found?

He hadn't touched it since that day in Dennie's office with Luna, but something pulled him toward it now, the thing—the "artifact," he'd called it that night—that was left after Dennie had died, had been torn apart. Still sipping his coffee, he headed into Dennie's office, opened the door reluctantly, not sure why he hesitated except for what always came back to him. He forced it from his mind this time, and went straight to the desk where he had put it.

Luna had told him to "drop it in a bag and put it in another room," but he hadn't done it; for the life of him, he couldn't imagine where else he would keep it. It belonged here, whatever it was. He picked it up, examining it again. What the hell was it? He'd thought it was part of a claw, but it was shaped differently, with its wiry fur. It repulsed him, but not so much as it had before. He turned it over, studying all sides of it, remembering how he'd touched it that first time, remembered the blood he thought he'd seen on its tip. Nothing now. Had he imagined it? He held it carefully, taking care with the tip. A fang? Tooth? Or nothing at all, he thought with amusement, recalling Luna's admonitions. Chances were, he'd attributed more to what Dennie called Luna's "sense of wonder" than he should have. Still, Luna's sense of things couldn't be ignored.

She could help him make sense of what Raine had told him, if she chose to. Luna had probably known for months, but telling a secret to Luna Loving Moore was as good as telling it to the dead; he knew that from his own experience, from Dennie's. I think I'd trust Luna with my life, Dennie told him once out of the blue, and he'd believed her, although he knew less about Luna and the life she'd led before they met her than he knew now.

He sat down in Dennie's chair, picked up the wedding photograph to study her face in detail, trying to see every tiny bit of her that could be captured in a photo— the hair, smile, eyes.

Why did it take your eyes?

Because I saw, my darling, Dennie said, answering his unspoken question, and the sound of her voice struck him dumb. He surveyed the room, forgetting for an instant where he was, what had happened, and then, just as quickly from nowhere a question formed in his mind:

What did you see?

My killer, of course.

The last thing she'd laid eyes on before she died, who-ever or whatever he or it had been—if he believed what Raine had said, and just thinking of Raine again brought a sigh that came so quickly and suddenly from so deep inside, he hadn't felt it coming. Sitting now in the clarity of daylight, away from the enchantment of the night, from her smell and touch, he wondered if he could be-lieve any of it—Davey changing, the thing chasing them. Unbelievable. That's what it was. But why had she lied to him? Because he'd imagined there was more there than there had been. Because she didn't have the courage to love him back. Because—

Because I saw.

Dennie's voice again, yet not so clear this time, coming from within himself, calling him away from his thoughts of Raine, bringing him back to this room, his question. Saw what? The killer? Or the truth? Was that what she was telling him, if she was telling him anything at all, if he wasn't losing his mind?

He slammed the drawer closed with so much force, he nearly knocked the photograph off the desk; leaving the office, he slammed that door, too, then headed into the kitchen. Dennie's kitchen—where he had kissed Raine, from where they'd left to make love, with Den-nie's blessing. Despite himself, he smiled because he re-alized that even from her grave, Dennie would have made it clear if he'd crossed some kind of line with the wrong kind of woman.

Later when he asked himself why he'd decided so suddenly to listen again, he realized it must have been the kitchen as much as anything else—as much as hearing Dennie's voice—*thinking* he heard Dennie's voice—as much as trying to find out answers to what Raine had told him. But there was a purpose to it this time when he pulled his laptop from the briefcase underneath his desk and plugged it in. He was in work mode when he sat down at this desk, his own territory, his space for preparing lesson plans, correcting flawed homework, paying bills; this was business now. He was listening for a reason, not for the sheer pleasure of hearing her voice and her laughter, for snatching her back from the dead.

Because I saw.

He was determined now to see it himself, whatever she told him she'd seen. Where to start? On the day she left him—was stolen from him. April 18. He slipped the earphones over his ears and heard her voice:

My subject is late. Our appointment was for nine
A.M., but an hour has passed and I've heard nothing.
A loss of nerves is often the case in matters such as
this, particularly when one considers the consequence
for betrayal of these "sacred" oaths. I hope that the
information offered will be worth my time and the fee
I've offered to pay and that there will be no objection
to my taping our interview. I am eager—yet strangely
wary.

The doorbell rang in the distance; the tape recorder was turned off. Then Dennie and someone else, sitting from far away, began to speak. Where were they talking?

Was it the other side of the room? At her desk, across from her? The voice was hushed, gruff. Woman or man? He couldn't tell. Dennie's voice was strained and tense. Not like her at all. Was it fear or anticipation that he heard?

—*Thank you for coming. I know this is difficult for you.*
—*Nothing must go from here.*
—*You object to being recorded?*
—*Nothing must go from here!*
—*It will be only for research. I need to keep records. Accurately.*
—*Fields have eyes and woods have ears.*
—*What do you mean by that?*
—*(no answer)*
—*I won't use your name.*
—*You don't know my name.*
—*Then I can't use it, can I?*

A nervous laugh. Dennie's.

—*May I ask you something? Why did you agree to do this interview? Was it the money?*
—*No.*
—*Then why?*
—*You will know in time.*

Cade turned up the volume, trying to hear the voice from far away, still unable to determine who was speaking. Woman? Man? Old? Young? Dennie gave no hint of identity, age, or gender.

Tape recorder, turned off again as abruptly as before. Who had turned it off? The subject? Dennie? He snatched off his earphones. Unwilling to hear what came next. Then put them on again, knowing he had no choice but to listen to the end—through the silences, through Dennie's discomfort, to whatever was said or wasn't. How much time elapsed before they began again? It was impossible to know. Dennie began again.

—*Why did you come here? To this town?*
—*A calling.*
—*Calling? What do you mean?*
—*A duty to keep what is mine.*
—*And what is yours?*
—*If it lives, it will kill me. It is his duty as it is mine.*
—*And who is he?*

A pause. Cade could hear Dennie's breath. She was afraid, he was sure of that now. Five minutes. Six. Before the voice came back again. Dennie now, her voice calmly probing.

—*There are some things I've read in the books about this . . . your ability, your skill, and the mythology surrounding it that I was hoping you could verify. You can nod your head if you want to if you don't want me to record what you say.*

Silence. Was there a nod? Dennie would note it, have filled in the rest when she typed it up.

—I've read the power began during the horror of the
Long Walk, when the U.S. Army backed by the
government forced your people, the Navajo, at
gunpoint—women, children, the most vulnerable
among you—to leave your homes in Arizona and
walk to New Mexico. That your people were starved,
beaten, children and pregnant women savagely
whipped.

   My people, too, experienced such horror.

   I've read that the . . . gifted people like yourself . . .
among them learned to change their shape to be able
to flee unseen from the guns and whips of your
oppressors. Is that true?

The voice was clear but deep, and there was bitter-
ness in the words.

   —There is much truth in that.
   —Can you read my thoughts?

A shifting of papers on Dennie's desk. Silence. Had it
been a nod? A smile.

   —It is said that you can make any voice your own.
Could you do that with me? Can you show me?
   —It is said that you can make any voice your own.
Could you do that with me? Can you show me?

The sound of it taking Dennie's voice like that, using
Dennie's words stopped his heart, and a chill went straight
through him.

*—It is said that white ash on a silver bullet can
destroy you. Is that true?*
*—A silver bullet? For vampires. Werewolves. Not
for us.*
*—I thought it was a stake through the heart for
vampires.*

Dennie trying for a joke? The laughter that came was
loud, dismissive.

*—Silver won't work. Not by itself, anyway. Try it if
you want to.*
—Should I be prepared to use it?

Dennie chuckled again, but it was forced and preten-
tious. She quickly changed the subject.

—How does it feel when you . . . change?
—I will show you when we meet again.
*—And when will that be? I'm not sure how to
interpret that. The look you just gave me.*

Dennie's words felt like a spike of ice driven through
him. They had met again, as it said they would.

He sat at his desk, unable to move, then played the
recording again—once and then twice—listening for
something he might have missed, listening as Dennie
might have done, and then turned it off. He considered
erasing it, forever getting rid of the voice that hadn't
been there, but he knew better than that. This was where
Dennie had led him, and he had to follow.

Because I saw, my darling.

He had it seen it, too, heard it now, and he could never forget it. The Jim Beam called him. He could feel the quick, pleasurable burn of it as it hit his throat, the warmth it brought to his belly as it headed there through his chest. The sweetness of it. He closed his eyes against it, his mouth, his nose, and pictured Dennie in his mind, before it had butchered her and destroyed his life, and in that instant, even before the thought had left him, he knew what he had to do.

Dennie's books. Dennie's notes.

He no longer doubted what Raine had told him. It had come back for his wife, and he knew now it would come back for her and her son like she'd said it would. He'd heard it himself, that dog that Dennie must have heard, and opened the door just to check because that was her way with all lost things.

I will show you when we meet again.

And it had shown her, too, in those moments before she died. She had mentioned the white ash on a silver bullet in passing and it had scoffed at the silver, but not the ash. Had she known more about killing them than she'd said? That must have been so, because Dennie's research was always meticulous; she wouldn't have asked the question unless she knew the answer.

Her office held no fear for him now, and he began with the notes on her desk, reading each and then starting with the three folders stuffed with transcriptions from blogs, each label identifying its subject: SKIN-WALKERS, WEREWOLVES, SHAPE-SHIFTING.

"My God, Dennie! What the hell were you into?" he

said aloud, angry and at the same time amused. The blogs gave nothing, mostly ramblings and half-baked theories from writers who used only one name or an odd pseudonym: Witch Hazel, Wolf's Breath, Dancer of Death. He doubted she'd taken them seriously, if you could take any of this stuff seriously, he thought, then chastised himself for his doubts. If he hadn't been so doubtful, so dismissive, maybe she would have told him about what she was doing, maybe she'd still be . . . No, don't go there, he told himself. But these blogs, some with e-mail addresses and claims to special knowledge, may have been where she got her subject's name. She would never have told him.

Dennie was a scholar, so he turned next to her bookcases, scanned the volumes on skin-walkers and werewolves stacked one upon the other in random order: *Some Kind of Power: Navajo Children's Skinwalker Narratives*, M. K. Brady; *Meeting the Medicine Men: An Englishman's Travels Among the Navajo*, C. Langley; *Werewolves, Shapeshifters and Skinwalkers*, K. Marika; *Navaho Witchcraft*, C. Kluckhohn. Piles of them, some dusty with wear—gotten from God knew where—some clearly self-published, others long out of print.

One in particular littered with Post-its caught his attention: *The Secretive Life of the Skin-walker*, A. S. Doggett. It was a slim black volume of a hundred or so pages published in the 1930s by a press long gone. Short passages were underlined on nearly every page, and he eagerly searched for the answers he knew must be there and finally found the passages marked on various pages with Post-its and highlighted with the pink highlighter Dennie favored.

These are beings who have gained power by committing an act of horror upon the members of their tribe, by breaking a cultural taboo that will forever deny them inclusion in the community. Often it is the murder of a blood relative.

It is believed that they steal the skin of another human being and absorb parts of that person into their person. It is believed they steal the soul or sight of a victim by the theft of their heart or eyes. They are considered the most evil of the supernatural beings, homicidal and violent to their very core.

Although they can change or shift into many creatures, the dire wolf, now extinct, or a wolfish dog is their favorite. They also adapt the habits of these creatures. They kill their victims only when they are alone.

Anger, greed, envy, and revenge are the emotions that spur their attacks. It is believed that blood once spilled must be revenged.

The skin-walker, as the wolf or vicious dog, is territorial and will not allow another of its kind to live within its territory, which can extend from forty to four hundred miles. It will seek and kill interlopers, first locating, stalking, encountering, and finally rushing to the kill in much the manner of the animal it emulates.

According to old legend, the best way to kill the creature is to scream its human name, then shoot it with a silver bullet dipped in white ash. It is also said one can defeat the creature's power by making it speak a loved one's name while in animal form, thus causing *it to lose forever its ability to shift. If the creature remains unchanged, its evil runs too deep and it will die.*

Dennie had tried to kill it. She must have shot once, then twice, aiming for its head but didn't know its name so it had made no difference. Her instincts told her to load the gun with bullets and she'd done that, her father's gun, that old .38 found beside her on that terrible day. There had been no gunfire residue on her hands because there were no hands left, no bullets in the barrel or anywhere in the room, and if she'd wounded something, it had left no blood.

By the time Cade was ten, his father had taught him to shoot. Hunting was one of the things they did together, but they'd stopped going after his father in a drunken rage pointed a Saturday night special at his mother because she wouldn't turn down the TV. But Cade wasn't scared of guns. He didn't like them but he knew how to handle one, and he handled this one with ease. God knew he'd been taught to do it, and seen his father do it—lock and load— find your stance, aim, shoot.

Dennie had shown him five silver bullets that day, he was sure of that, because he remembered her crack all those months ago about five bullets being enough to kill anything that growled in the dark, about how they'd cost a pretty penny. He was only half-listening, hadn't thought much about it then, but silver bullets would have had to be specially made for this old .38. She'd taken the time to find out who made them and bought them because she'd thought she might need to use them.

Why hadn't she told him? He answered the question for himself: Because she didn't want to hear his relentless, dismissive teasing. He placed the gun and the three bullets left back in the manila envelope, leaving them on top of the desk.

Then he went into the kitchen to call Raine.

14

raine

I woke up before Cade and lay there watching him sleep like I used to do with Davey when he was a kid, like I used to do with Elan. I thought about how vulnerable men looked when they were laid out like little boys, breathing deep and soft, defenseless against any evil that lurked and snuck their way. Elan's voice came back to me then, that last night we stayed together, Davey kicking hard inside my womb.

Time for him to come out, he'd said, and he rolled on top and kissed me, careful not to hurt the baby, although I'd told him a dozen times that if babies came out that easy, nobody would carry to term, but he was always so gentle about everything, one of the reasons I loved him so. We'd made love then, silently and soft, so as not to wake Anna in the other room, so sure that our love and the baby would make things good for the rest of our lives, no sense of what horror would meet us, crouching in the dark, awaiting its chance. Anna had warned us to take care before the baby was born, and we'd listened but ignored her like we always did, so sure that our love would protect us from everything that could hurt us.

Why hadn't he told me about the dangers? Did he think I would leave him? And maybe I would have, looked out for myself and our baby, gotten away while I could. That had been part of my grief, anger at him for saying nothing, for keeping the secret that he carried inside him, the threat that would destroy him and try to kill our child.

Cade shifted in his sleep, and my thoughts came back to the man beside me, as gentle in his own way as Elan had been. I doubted he believed what I'd told him, although I hoped he did. I doubted he would forgive me now, but I hoped he would do that someday, too. He stirred, reaching out for me, his arm falling against my breast, and I picked up his hand, careful not to wake him, kissed each of his fingertips and eased my body away from him and out of his bed.

Quickly, as soundlessly as I could, I scooped my clothes off the floor and hurried into the bathroom down the hall to change, noticing for the first time the layout of the house. Two bedrooms on this floor, separated by the large bathroom I'd entered. A room for a baby, that second room, the child that would never be born, and for that instant, I thought about climbing back into bed with him, being a part of the life he'd lost that he had seen me returning to him. I had no doubt that grief played into how he felt about me, how could it not? But I knew—and feared—that all I could bring him, me and my son—who was changing daily into someone neither of us would know—was more grief, adding to his sorrow.

I'd seen scrap paper on his desk earlier and I crept into the living room to write a short note explaining as much as I could, then went back upstairs and placed it on the bureau so he would see it when he woke up. He slept soundly, his breath even and peaceful. I bent down and kissed him lightly on the lips, whispering good-bye; then I left the house from the back door, glancing once around the kitchen and locking the door behind me.

It was dawn, and the world was bathed in the pink of first light. I paused between Luna's and Cade's homes, pulling the morning air deep inside me as I tried to rid myself of doubts that remained. A new day with new beginnings—each one a chance to renew. I squeezed between the bushes, sat down in the swing, rocking back and forth, letting its rhythm calm me as I waited for the sun to come up.

A new day was here, and I could define how I would live it in any way I choose, a new start for me and Davey, wherever we ended up. I promised myself that I would find a way out of this for both of us, until he was old enough to battle what I now knew he must. But he wasn't old enough yet; I was sure of that, despite what secrets Anna had whispered, perhaps still did. I would find a way.

As soon as Davey was awake, we'd go. It never took him long to get over his anger; he'd be fine by the time he got up. Packing would be easy. I'd stored our bags in Luna's attic, and Davey had outgrown most of his clothes anyway. He'd changed so much in the past few months, I wondered if he'd even want to bring the things he'd packed in the spring. We'd leave what we could with

Luna to send to us when we were settled. We'd head north this time. I'd heard the schools were good in Massachusetts, and with Cade's tutoring over the summer, he would find his way. He'd need to say good-bye to Cade, in his own way, or perhaps he'd decide that was too painful, like it had almost been for me. When we settled, when I was sure we were safe, he could write him. Things would work out; they always did. Because as Davey got older, so did the thing that stalked us. He had youth on his side, and if he never fought, never was drawn into a blood battle with it, he would simply outlive it, and that part of his nature might never come out, despite all Anna's warnings and talk of revenge.

But even as I imagined it, I knew it could never be. This was part of Davey and it always would be—boy, youth, man—but he and I together would find a way to control it. This move would give us time, but I knew it would not be the last one, not for a while. I peered through the hedges at Cade's house and remembered the drawings I made of the flowers the day that Davey, so terrified and weeping, had told me it found us. He hadn't heard the dog since then; at least, he hadn't mentioned it. But I had seen it at the carnival, pretending to be something else, and as the sun rose and shone on the backyard, I remembered something else Anna had told me.

They fool you because they move faster than any living thing you can imagine—so fast, it seems they can be in two places at once. One thing one time and someone entirely different each time you look. Because they take over anyone they want to. All they need to do is stare at someone hard to absorb that person into them, become them, wear their skin like it's their own.

And that was what it had done.

Luna was sitting at the kitchen table, drinking a cup of tea, when I came in through the back door.

"I thought you might still be at Cade's."

"No. I left before morning. I've been sitting outside for a while, just swinging and waiting for the day to start good so I can wake up Davey."

She held up her cup, as if toasting me. "So it's one for the road?"

"I guess so," I said, more sadly than I'd meant to, knowing this would be the last time we'd be together like this. Luna turned the kettle on and measured tea into a pot.

"That old swing is going to miss you all, between the two of you, you gave it quite a workout. You know where you're going this time?" She was stirring honey into her tea and avoiding my eyes, and I didn't look into hers when I answered.

"Boston, maybe. Davey likes the Celtics, so maybe he'd like to go there. I don't know, Luna. So much has happened so fast—Cade, my feelings about him, and then that . . . thing showing up when she did."

"She?"

"I know who it is," I said, no longer avoiding her eyes. "I knew it when I saw her in that carnival, but I wasn't sure until you told me she was here."

"Doba."

"At first I thought it might be her father, because of the way he was shunned at Anna's funeral and maybe it was at first. He may have killed Elan, maybe the two of them did that together or maybe she killed him alone, but I'm sure it's her."

Luna drank her tea meditatively, taking little sips like it burned her lips, sipping at it like she had that Bloody Mary when I told her about Davey that night, but when she finally spoke this time, it wasn't with the conviction she'd had then, the certainty that we could beat it. Maybe she knew too much about what we were fighting, or maybe that gift they said everybody in our family had told her what I already knew.

Until we figure something out, she'd said that night, but it was different this time; things weren't to be figured out. She finished her tea, putting the cup neatly into its matching saucer. "It was a thumb," she said after a minute.

"A thumb?" I didn't get it at first, and then it came together for me as it must have for her.

"The thing in Dennie's office that looked like a piece of a claw, that's what it was. It was her thumb." Luna shook her head, slowly reprimanding herself, and I saw the sparkle of a tear in her eyes. "I should have known what the damn thing was when I saw it, Raine. I should have known it when it stood right there on my porch wearing that ring like your earrings, bragging about the loss of its thumb. Damned, filthy thing!" She dropped her head to her chest, as if scolding herself. "I let you down."

"No, Luna, never!" I hugged her, holding her tightly like I had my grandfather before he died, a child's hug, trying to offer her a bit of the comfort she'd offered me. The smell of ginger and cinnamon, which hung around

Luna in a fragrant cloud, made my throat tighten as I realized how much I'd miss her. "You did everything you could. Took us in. Looked after us. I've brought all this on you and Cade."

"Don't ever think that. You saved that man's life."

"Ruined it, more likely."

"No! You don't know what was going on before you came. I thought the sun would never come up for him again, and it did, even if it was just for a day or two, just enough to help things bloom."

This had been more a home to me than any of the other places I'd been, even with Anna, although I'd lived with her the longest. There was always an invisible threat in Anna's presence, a shadow of anxiety that loomed around her as faintly as the ginger and cinnamon floated around Luna. I'd joked once to Luna about what a good mother she'd be, and she'd shaken her head in protest. Woe be to any child who had me as mama, she'd told me. You have to have a good mother to be a good mother, and Geneva, bless her soul, nearly drove me crazy half the time. But you, Raine, you're the best mother that boy could hope for, she'd told me. I hoped she was right.

Luna got up and gathered the cups and put some bacon in a skillet for breakfast, and the smell and sound of it sizzling made me remember how hungry I was. "Thought I'd make some waffles today—he always loves those. Be a good way to get you two on your way."

I nodded, dreading facing Davey again. So I put it off a few more minutes, running what I'd say to him over again in my mind, except I'd said it so many times before, I knew it by heart. It was what I'd said to him that night after she showed up at Mack's and before that when we left South Jersey and now.

"Right after breakfast, you think?" Luna broke into my thoughts.

"Yeah, as soon as we're all packed. Can you ship things to us when we get settled?"

"You don't even have to ask me that. I guess you said your good-bye to Cade last night." A mischievous smile played briefly on her lips.

"I hope you're not expecting details." It was the first time I'd smiled that morning.

"Those last good-byes are always the sweetest," Luna said with a sly chuckle more to herself than to me, but her eyes darkened with sadness and I wondered how many sweet last good-byes, how many sad ones, she'd uttered in her lifetime. I knew far less of Luna than she knew of me. I regretted now that I hadn't taken the time to let her talk more about her life and whom she'd loved and lost. "You know you do have a couple of days of grace. It's only Monday, and if it's been like the other times, it will wait for the full moon to come, and that's not until Friday night—"

"No," I said, making my voice as gentle as I could because I knew Luna would miss us as much as we'd miss her. She nodded and turned back to her mixing bowl.

"Davey, come on downstairs. Breakfast is ready," Luna called from the stove as she poured batter into the waffle iron. "Waffles. Come get them while they're hot."

"I'll get him," I said, heading to the stairs. I needed to

start packing for both of us; Davey would have done nothing. I also needed to have a few words with him before he came downstairs. He could spend time with Luna—and with Cade, too—while I packed. It would be good for both of them. And I needed more time to myself, just to think.

I'm not sure what stopped me when I got to Davey's door. That sense that mothers have that says things aren't right, that makes the hair on the back of your neck bristle like some stranger's fingers grazing it. I said his name anyway, softly at first and then until I was yelling it. When there was no sound, no movement, I opened the door and saw what I already knew: He was gone.

The window was open, but only slightly, and I saw how he left, as some smaller animal—but not too small, he'd said at church that day, not too weak, not too easily conquered. Somehow, I kept from screaming as I searched for some clue I knew wasn't there, something besides his clothes in a pile on the bed, his glasses folded on his desk. I picked them up, hugged them to my breast as if they were part of him as a wild panic surged through me, coming with the sudden, terrible knowledge that I might never see him again. All my fears and dread had finally become real, and that was when the scream that had settled into the bottom of my stomach tore from my heart and out of my throat. I fell down on the edge of his bed and pulled his clothing to my face, trying to trap the scent of him forever inside me.

"Davey." I whispered his name this time, loving the feel of it on my lips. Davey. And suddenly I was aware of the scent of cinnamon and ginger, and the warm bulk of Luna as she grabbed me to her bosom, hugging me as I hugged Davey's clothing.

"I didn't know he would go, I should have . . . I didn't know . . ."

I didn't understand what she was saying, because I couldn't hear her. Had we sat there ten minutes? Fifteen, until Luna stood up, letting go of my hand. "He must have left right after I got back from Jocelyn's," she said. "I knocked on his door and he answered, and then I went to bed. I should have—" She stopped reminding herself of what she'd just told me. "I'm going to look around outside and see if I can find anything. He knew what he was doing when he left. Nothing got him, we can be thankful for that."

"How do you know that?" I wasn't able to look at her. I couldn't open my eyes.

"Because he left his glasses on his desk, and that could mean he'll be back for them, sooner or later. They weren't on the floor or smashed or broken. He knew what he was doing, where he was going." And there was no blood. No flesh ripped from his bone. Not like Elan or Dennie or Mack. Luna didn't have to say that, but I knew what she was thinking because some small part of me was thinking it, too, grateful for what little there was to be thankful for.

"But what if . . ." I couldn't bring myself to say it; saying it could make it happen.

"It won't," Luna said softly, but I knew she didn't know that any more than I did. "I'll see if there's anything outside. He opened the window, climbed out on the roof, jumped down . . ." She paused, and I knew she was thinking what had occurred to me: Whatever he'd changed into had the ability to jump, to spring from the window to the ground like an animal did. It was both a blessing and a curse.

He'd taken on the mantle with which Anna bethrothed him, but she wasn't here to guide him, nobody was but me, and I had no idea what he was up against. I was as helpless and vulnerable as he was. The fear crawled up my body and tightened my throat, and when it came out, it was a wail. I wasn't aware it had come out of me until Luna grabbed me again, gently shaking me, trying to bring me back to myself.

"Come down with me," she said. "Help me look outside."

"Let me stay here a few minutes, okay?"

Reluctantly, she nodded. "I'll be back up to check on you in a few."

I sat at Davey's desk, remembering him studying here, so intent on doing the homework Cade had given him to do, and thought about Sunday at the carnival, trying too hard to be a normal kid like all the others, but knowing that he never could be—that he carried Anna's, Elan's curse inside him. And finally he'd accepted it. Taken it on because he had no choice.

When the phone rang downstairs, my first thought was Davey. Maybe he had come back into himself, stuck somewhere with no clothes, cold and frightened. Had the cops picked him up, assumed he was some troubled runaway who had nowhere to go? Let him make one call. I ran downstairs, trying to get to the phone in the kitchen before whoever it was hung up.

"Davey!" I screamed into the receiver. Silence. Was he afraid to speak? Was someone stopping him from answering? "Is that you? Please answer me!"

"It's Cade. Isn't Davey there with you?"

I couldn't answer; I couldn't think of the words to tell him what had happened.

"Raine, are you there? Answer me, please!"

"Yes," I said because that one word took no energy.

"Davey is gone?"

"Yes."

"Can you tell me what happened?"

"I don't know," I managed to say, but the words came out muffled in a sob I couldn't control.

"Look, I know what you said, but I want to come over, is that okay? I need to see you and know what's going on with Davey. Maybe I can help you figure this thing out." He paused and then added, "I *know* I can help you figure this thing out."

I knew that even if I said no, he would have come anyway. I could hear the fear and worry in his voice. Davey and Cade had forged their own friendship that was separate from ours, the same as he and Mack had done.

"Raine?"

"Please come," was all I managed to say.

It seemed that before I hung up the phone, Cade was standing beside me in the kitchen, holding me to him, giving me as much of his strength as he could. Luna

210

came in shortly after that, and I could tell by the look on her face that she'd found nothing. I wasn't surprised. The three of us sat down at the kitchen table, and Luna made some tea—her remedy for whatever was ailing in the world, but nobody drank it and nobody spoke until Cade finally broke the silence and fear that hung over us.

"I know how we can kill it," he said.

15

cade

Thursday morning. Davey had been gone three days. There was nothing Cade could say, so he said nothing. All he could do was listen—to Raine's sobs, holding her as much as she would let him, rocking her like he remembered his mother had once rocked him—and how long in his past had that been? he wondered at one point. The most enduring remembrance he had of that poor woman was how she'd comforted him; he pulled it out now, as much as he recalled, to help him take care of Raine in her sorrow. Luna had suggested she spend nights with him, give Davey some time to "sneak back in," as she put it, so Raine had stayed at his place each night, praying that she'd go back to Luna's in the morning and find her son asleep in his bed. He hoped Luna was right but suspected she wasn't.

As much as Cade mistrusted cops, after twenty-four hours passed, he gently suggested they call them, report Davey as a runaway, see what they had to say. At least then it would be official, and the police would keep an eye out for him. Kids his age ran away all the time, and cops usually knew where to look. He'd talk to them, he'd said, tell them what happened. What he didn't say was that he didn't want her to get hysterical and start talking about some creature that was after them both. It can't do any harm, he'd explained, and if you think something is chasing him, then—Raine's glare, like he'd slapped her in the mouth, made him stop mid-sentence. Have you forgotten what I told you, about the way Davey can shift, about why he has shifted? Cops won't do any good. They'll just make things worse. It was the first time she'd ever raised her voice at him, and the sound of it coming from someone who was always so gentle stunned him. So he'd let it go. Not mentioned the cops again. Just said whatever she wanted to hear.

He had begun to believe what she told him about the creature. He'd heard it for himself, the way it talked to Dennie, how it could be killed, but he didn't fully understand why it was after Davey and Raine. And he couldn't yet bring himself to believe that Davey could become what Raine had said. Or maybe he just didn't want to believe it. It was more likely that the boy was just mad at his mother because he was sick and tired of being pulled every which way into some new town every couple of years. He wanted to stay put. He'd probably run away to scare her, prove himself, and get his own way. Boys did that sometimes; he sure had. He just hoped he wouldn't regret not pushing the cop thing.

I know because I always do.

That was all Raine had said when he pressed her about her fears, and he knew now that wasn't enough. When he saw Davey again—and he was sure he would see him again—he'd find a way to talk to him about the things that Raine had told him. He'd get some answers from Davey, make him fill in the blanks his mother had left out. And he had answers himself now, but he knew Raine wasn't ready to hear them yet. All she needed was comforting, so that was what he gave her.

They talked at night, until dawn sometimes. She'd tell him what she could remember about Elan and his family, and he tried to make sense of the things she told him. Mostly it was about Anna, who he hadn't realized played such an influential role in Davey's life, and who Raine believed had ties to him even from the grave. It sounded insane, but then he remembered Dennie, and how he'd doubted, even ridiculed things she'd said to him. If only he'd listened to her, so he listened to Raine now, saying nothing but listening to her as Dennie would have.

He held Raine as much as she would let him, comforting her as he could with body, mind, whatever he could think of to stop her from crying, or from screaming when he thought she was asleep. Had what had come for Davey finally gotten him? What if her son was dead? He's not dead, Cade would tell her with as much conviction as he could muster, but the longer Davey was gone, the more worried he became, too. He brought her as much comfort as he could but not what she needed. She needed her son, and he was no good at that.

It was Luna, bringer of meals and mysticism, who finally gave her hope.

"It won't come out again until Friday night. Remember I told you that?" she'd said Wednesday night. "Wherever

Davey is, he's safe until then. I know enough about the other world to say that." They were sitting in the kitchen and Luna had brought over dinner. Not the veggie soup and healthy bread she was prone to make, but the kind Cade liked—chicken-fried steak, mashed potatoes, collard greens, flaky biscuits—and he was wolfing down the food like he wouldn't see tomorrow. Raine, nibbling timidly on a biscuit, touched nothing. Strong emotions always made Cade hungry, he'd known that since he was a kid; curiosity forced his fork back to his plate.

"Other world?"

"You know what I'm talking about," Luna snapped with a glance in Raine's direction, who had looked up quickly as if she hadn't quite heard Luna's words.

"If anything happens, it will come then, so you'd best prepare yourself like I told you before. Remember I told you that." Luna fixed her gaze on Raine, and she nodded as if she understood. "You're not going to be able to leave like you thought. You're going to have to stay until that moon comes out and wait for your boy to do what he's determined to do."

"Will somebody tell me what the hell you two are talking about?" said Cade.

And Luna did, and as she explained, he remembered there was to be a full moon the night it had slaughtered Dennie. That was why he had brought the wine, that was why they had planned to make love that night, because the moon was full and Dennie loved to make love in moonlight.

Sorrow overtook him as he relived that night, and he could feel his heart drop deep into the place where it went sometimes, where he hadn't wanted to pull it out until he met Raine. He studied her now, her anguish as deeply etched in her face as it was in his heart.

A silence thick with dread overcame the three of them as Cade listened to the house, trying to identify any noise that didn't belong there, that might do them harm, but there were only the sounds he half heard every day: the septic tank pumping groundwater from the basement, a clock ticking in the hall, the hum of the air conditioner in his bedroom. And he listened to Raine breathing—holding her breath, then letting it out slowly in one long exhalation.

The thought came to Cade suddenly, and he held on to it, not sure how much good it would do to mention it now, though it had been on his mind since Monday after he read the passages in the book. That was why he'd called Raine, of course, to tell her he knew how to kill it. He'd looked for the chance to explain it, but every thought he'd had for the past three days concerned how best to comfort her. But this was something else entirely that had come to him last night, and he'd let the thought bloom in his mind.

You've got to lure him in, play him for a fool. Let him have your bishop so you can get his queen. You've got to see at least four moves in the future, four moves down the board, so you can win.

Those had been his father's words to him, and he'd told them to Davey, and he was sure that was what Davey was going to do. Davey would try to take whatever was stalking him by surprise. He would lure it away from his mother and Luna. Davey was comfortable here, and this was where he would try to kill it. Whatever she said about Davey "shifting," as she called it, whether it was true or not, Davey knew the threat the creature posed to him and Raine, and he was ready to meet the challenge. Wasn't that how boys became men, the whole point of the rites of passage boys went through in indigenous cultures? Dennie had been an expert on that, too, when he told her about the risks he had taken at twelve and thirteen. How he sought out danger sometimes, just to spite his drunken father, his dead mother.

A rite of passage. Davey knew he was the bait, for whatever the reason, and he would try to be the killer. What Davey didn't know was that he couldn't do it alone. Raine would need to play a part, too, if they were going to defeat it. Cade sensed that Davey wouldn't go back to Luna's house; he would come here, where the creature had killed Dennie. It was just a matter of waiting.

He glanced at Raine's face—so dull and tight, it looked as if it were carved from stone. Best to wait for Davey to come, and he was certain he would now, as sure as he was of the chess moves Davey always played. If Davey came tonight or tomorrow, he would tell Raine what had happened, and the two of them could talk about what to do. At least she would know her son was safe—for the time being, anyway.

Luna picked up her head as if she had heard something odd, and Cade wondered if she had, if he'd miscalculated and things would happen sooner than he'd thought. But she nodded at him, as if acknowledging something he'd said. Luna always seemed to know what was on his mind.

"I could use some company tonight, Raine, if it's okay with you and Cade." Raine's eyes were empty. "Might help just to sit in his room tonight. Be around his things. Might bring you some comfort."

Raine simply nodded, saying nothing. They all stood up together, Cade studying Luna as he often did, as curious about her as ever.

"Come on, let's go, then. Cade, you can finish up this food, put it in the fridge, you can have it tomorrow."

Cade nodding, walked them to the back door and through the bushes into Luna's backyard.

"I won't get any sleep tonight," Raine said before she went inside.

"Yes, you will. Have Luna fix you one of her teas. We'll see what happens tomorrow."

She managed a smile, but it was filled with woe, and Cade knew that she thought nothing would change; he hoped she was wrong. He went back to his own house, allowed himself the Bud Light he kept tucked in the back of the refrigerator away from Luna's watchful eyes, and sat on the couch in the living room, patiently waiting for the boy to show up.

Davey came through the back door as he always did. It was almost one. Cade had fallen asleep, a dreamless, restless sleep filled with anxiety. The sound of the screen door snapping shut shocked him awake. He sat up, wondering if it was Raine or Luna, and then suddenly afraid it might be something else. Fully awake, he sat up, his body stiff as he listened.

"Cade, you upstairs?" Davey's voice.

"Where the hell have you been?" Cade ran into the kitchen, stopping short at the sight of the naked eleven-year-old sitting at his kitchen table.

"Sorry about this," said Davey.

"No problem. Let me get you some clothes, then I'm going to call your mama."

"No! Not yet." Davey's tone told Cade to wait, so he nodded reluctantly to show he would. Best to find out what the boy had to say. It was going on one in the morning, and if Raine wasn't asleep, she would be soon.

He found some clean sweatpants and a T-shirt at the bottom of his drawer and grabbed some socks on the way down. This would have to do for now. Davey pulled them on quickly, then settled back down at the table.

"You hungry? You been gone for damn near three days."

"Yeah."

"Here," Cade said as he pulled Luna's leftovers from the refrigerator. "Eat this first, and then you got to tell me what's going on."

Cade watched as Davey shoved food into his mouth, barely chewing. When he was finished, he pushed his plate away like any other hungry kid would. Cade could see the boy was tired, but he needed to get what he could out of him first before he went to sleep. To his surprise, Davey stood and headed for the door.

Cade jumped up to stop him. "Not yet."

"But, Cade—"

"You owe me some kind of explanation. Showing up here butt-naked, sitting at my kitchen table."

"It's coming for me. It got Mack and now it's coming for me, and Mom if she's around. That's why she can't be around."

"What are you talking about?"

"You know what I'm talking about."

Cade paused, then acknowledged that he did; there was no sense denying it. "Where are your clothes?"

"At Luna's house."

"So you've been running around the street naked?"

"No. It wasn't me. . . . I was . . . something else."

"And what does that mean?"

"I can't tell you!" Davey's voice rose to an angry pitch that he'd never heard before.

"I need to know what is going on. All of it."

"But I got to go—"

"Why?"

"Didn't Mom tell you about me? Didn't she tell you?"

The anguish in Davey's eyes tore at Cade's heart. It was clear he was going to cry. Boys his age didn't let themselves cry easily, especially around other men. If they were going to talk, it was going to be man to man. The way he never spoke to his father, the way he knew Davey would never be able to speak to his own.

"I need you to tell me exactly what happens to you. I need to know what you plan to do about it," he said, almost adding "son," surprised how easily it had nearly flowed off his tongue.

Davey sat back down at the table and Cade sat across from him, studying his face, carefully looking for any sign of what Raine said he could become. But he could see nothing except the boy he'd known all summer, the one he'd grown to care about.

"You sure you want to know?" That was Davey's wise-cracking tone, covering up the tears that had come to his eyes, and it made Cade smile.

"Think I can't take it?"

Davey paused, searching Cade's face—for what, Cade wasn't sure—and he remembered the words Dennie had written about them not breaking the oath of silence that was bound within them. Davey had never told anyone his secrets, not even his mother.

Davey smirked. "Naw, I know you can take it. I don't think you'll believe me."

"Try me," Cade said, rocking back in his chair to listen.

"So my mom didn't tell you about me? About, you know—the shifting shit?" He was procrastinating.

"Some of it."

"Can I have something to drink, first, like some water or juice or something?"

Cade got ice out of the freezer, put it in a tall glass, and topped it off with apple juice.

Davey gulped down half before he began. "It's easier now, even though I, you know, shift into bigger stuff, like my grandma said I would. I can do it now just by thinking about it, by seeing something that I want to be and making my body become it. Grandma said that when I get older, I can switch into people, like walk in their skin and shit, you know like—" He stopped suddenly, dropped his eyes, not wanting to go on.

"Don't you have to kill them first, though, to slip into them?" Cade took all feeling and judgment out of his voice, making himself look the boy in the face, remembering he was talking to Davey, the eleven-year-old he had taught to play chess, who liked to drink apple juice, whom he was sure he could love like a son if given half a chance.

"I don't know," he said. "Mama Anna said that part would come, too, when I was ready. But I don't want that part to come, Cade. I don't want to be that."

Cade sighed, not sure where to go from there, what to tell the boy except what sounded like boilerplate advice, the kind you gave anyone who didn't want to walk down the path they were headed. The kind he wished somebody had told him, the kind of things Dennie had said so many times to him that his voice sounded like hers.

"You always have a choice, Davey. You have what they call free will that—"

"That's bullshit, and you know it," Davey said, not hiding his irritation. "I woke up this morning with blood on my hands, all over my body."

"Blood!" Cade didn't try to hide his shock.

"Sure you want to hear this?"

"Yeah, I told you I did!"

"Okay, yeah, blood! Yeah. I must have killed something—a squirrel, a cat, something—and I didn't know I did it. That's what this thing is, Cade. I don't have any control over it. You want to know what it's like? It's like being in a fucking nightmare where you see yourself becoming something you don't want to be, where it's you but it's not. I'm scared I'm going to hurt my mom or Luna. Hurt you. Or even Pinto. He's little, and even though he can't talk, he knows what I am. I almost changed in front of him. What if I hurt him?"

Neither of them spoke awhile as Davey stared at the table, hiding what Cade knew was shame.

"So how does it stop?" he asked, going to the refrigerator and getting out another bottle of apple juice. He always kept two on ice for Davey. His hand was shaking when he gave it to him, and he hoped Davey hadn't noticed.

"It just does."

"And so you just showed up here naked as a jaybird because whatever had taken over you just decided to let you go?"

"That's about it." There was a glimmer of amusement in Davey's eyes. "Jaybird? What the fuck is a jaybird?"

"Watch your mouth. You been throwing around so many 'fucks,' it's like you just learned the word. Jaybird? A crazy bird that shows up naked at somebody's house at one in the morning."

Davey shrugged, and Cade, recognizing the universal preteen sign that nothing more was going to be said, let it go. He glanced at the clock—it was two-thirty now, and Cade knew that even if Raine had managed to fall asleep he had to wake her. "It's time for me to call your mom. She's worried sick about you."

"Can I talk to her first?" Cade handed him the phone. "Alone?"

"Sure. Of course."

Cade went into the living room and sat on the couch, but there was no door to close. He knew if he listened carefully, he could hear every word the boy said, and so he did.

16

raine

You've got to let me go, that's all, Mom, you've got to let me do what I need to do.

Davey . . .

There's nothing you can do about it. Why can't you just accept me for who I am, what I am? Mama Anna did, she knew—if my dad was alive, he would have. He would have told me like Mama Anna did, that this was my destiny.

Destiny! Do you even know what the word means?

I know close enough.

You never knew your father, he would not say that! You can't do it alone.

Don't you understand? I don't have a choice. And if it kills me, I don't care. I'd rather die than live like the kind of freak I am. Kill me if it doesn't. Promise me you will!

Davey! Don't say that. Don't you dare say that!

But that's how I feel.

How do you know it will come?

Because tonight is when it's supposed to come, and it has been here before and it knows I'll be waiting for it.

Davey was gone by the time I ran through the bushes to
Cade's house. He'd left the back door open, getting away
as fast as he could. I wondered if those would be the last
words he would say to me, about wanting me to kill him,
and that tore into my heart as nothing ever had before.

He must have known it from the beginning, from the
day he walked into that room with Pinto carrying on like
he had that he would meet the thing again, that something evil had happened there, as Luna had put, and
sooner or later that evil would come back for him.

Cade was in the living room when I rushed into the
house. He met me in the kitchen, taking me in his arms.

"I heard what Davey said, but you've got to remember
that he's just a kid, and kids say dumb things. They think
they're stronger than they are." The way he held me and
spoke to me made me remember the first time I saw
him, how I'd known he was the kind of man who could
carry any kind of bags you brought with you; he'd already picked up mine.

"He says he has to fight it on his own," I said, still not
believing him. "But he's not strong enough yet—even
Anna with all her craziness wouldn't want that to happen. You saw what it did to Dennie, I know what it did
to Elan—I can't let that happen to my son, Cade, no
matter what he thinks he has to do."

"And we won't," Cade said, leading me back to the
couch, and I fell back onto it, not sure if I could stand up
again. "We won't let it kill him."

But even though his words were bravely spoken, I knew he was as scared as me.

"How did he look? What did he say?"

"He ate a lot. I gave him some clothes."

"Clothes? He needed clothes?"

"Well—" He glanced away, not meeting my eyes. "—when he changes, shifts . . . he goes down to his skin. Other than that, sitting around naked in my kitchen, he was the same kid. Joking around, easy to talk to."

"He shifted?" It surprised yet also eased my fears; he trusted Cade enough for that, and I knew with certainty that Cade believed me now; he knew what I was up against.

"Told me how it felt, what scared him about it, but I didn't see him do it. He said he needed to shift back so he could . . ." He didn't finish the sentence, but I knew what it was. In order to fight what he had to fight. In order to meet his "destiny."

"Tonight?"

"That's what he said."

It had come down to this. All my running and hiding and looking for ways to keep us safe. All those days of not being able to catch my breath out of fear, of keeping secrets I didn't want to keep. Destiny, as Anna had called it, the one she had predicted and he now embraced. I didn't know I was crying until Cade wiped the tears off my face, holding my hands until they stopped. It was then that he went into Dennie's office and brought back an old book with a tattered cover and a manila envelope with a gun and three bullets tucked inside.

❧

At four, I went through the bushes into Luna's backyard to get white ash from the gardening supplies she kept under the porch. Luna came into the yard as I was opening the jar.

"Did you actually think I would forget what tonight is, what that child is facing?" she said, not bothering to hide her annoyance.

I spooned the ash into a cup, avoiding her eyes.

"So what is it, white ash? Will that do it?"

"White ash and silver bullets."

"Yeah, silver is good for every damn thing, and I've heard white ash can be handy, too. Mama used to toss it around every now and then, but it was never one of her basics. I keep it on hand to sprinkle outside just in case it works—like a good luck charm when you fly on a plane."

I nodded and kept on spooning.

"You think I'm going to let you face that damn thing on your own?"

I stopped spooning and faced her. "We'll need you to be there after it's over one way or the other—that's when I will really need you," I said as gently as I could. "This is between me, Davey, and the creature. It always has been. Cade is there because it picked his home, killed his wife, but this is my battle, Luna, mine and Davey's. Just like you said it was."

"When did I say that?"

I softened my voice and reminded her. "Don't you remember that first night I stayed with you? What you said about standing my ground? About not running for the rest of my life?" Her lips parted in what couldn't be called a smile, but I knew that she did remember. "It's Davey's fight, but it's mine, too, I'm making it mine because I'm his mother, and it killed the one person in my life I loved as much as him."

We stood there, me knowing this might be the last moment of peace I ever had. I wondered if I should thank her for all she'd done for me, what she'd given us without even realizing it.

"I'll be there when you need me," she said, hugging me to her like she had that first day in the church, giving me her strength, allowing me to take as much as I needed.

When I came back, Cade stood by the kitchen door, uneasy and anxious. His face was tight with tension, fear, but loosened as we read aloud the passages from the book that Dennie had left us, and I thought of it like that now. Her gift to him, to us.

Dennie had underlined certain things with pink highlighter, and I tried to memorize each word about how to kill it, and I felt close to Dennie then, too, this woman who had left the clues that might save my son's life. But I was frightened by the sentence, about the evil running too deep to cure, and how he could remain unchanged. I tried not to let those words into my head.

We sat down at the kitchen table and he got out the bullets and the gun. I'd never seen silver bullets, and I was struck by their beauty—as shiny and heavy as good jewelry. Use enough ash to coat them well, Cade reminded me, make sure they're completely covered.

Cade had spent most of the morning at gun shops, buying bullets and a silencer from a dealer he knew so I could practice and nobody would report us to the cops. I remembered some of what my grandfather had told me all those years ago. About how to hold it, how to point, but this was bigger and heavier than the gun my grandfather had owned. My hand shook when I held it. Cade showed me how to center it in the web of my right hand, use the left to hold it steady, he told me, thumbs relaxed, find your stance, then aim. Breathe to relax, to control it. Don't squeeze it like a piece of fruit, hold it light, lock it light. And shoot.

He'd loaded it with the bullets he'd bought, put the silencer on, and I practiced in the backyard, hitting garbage bags packed with rags and newspapers stacked against the garage door. I was a good shot, my grandfather used to say, and Cade said it now, too, better than he was when he'd started. I believed him because I had to.

"Do you want me to take care of this for you? Please let me do it," he begged again and again, and each time I told him no. It was my fight, not his. I didn't tell him the real reason I didn't want him to be in the room with me. If the thing killed Davey, I would go for it myself, let it kill me along with my son. I didn't want to live if it took my boy; it was as simple as that. I thought I might be in love with Cade—I was pretty sure he was with me—but I'd had too much grief for one lifetime. I would shoot until I ran out of bullets, then throw my body at it.

"Are you sure you know its name?" Cade asked when we took a break. I was too nervous to drink a sip of water. "That's the most important thing. Dennie didn't, and—"

"I think I do."

"Think isn't good enough, Raine. You need to be sure. Dennie—"

"Doba. Its name is Doba."

"Are you sure?"

I nodded like I was, but I wasn't. Could it be her father, the uncle whose name nobody would say? Maybe it was him, not her. No. It was her. It had to be. She'd been at the carnival, hadn't she? She'd waited for us in Luna's back-yard. It was she who knew where we were, who had shown up at Mack's that time. She was the strongest because she was the youngest, and Davey was younger than she; she feared him because of that.

Yet there was still a shade of doubt.

We went back outside to practice some more. Aim. Say the name. Shoot. He must have told me that a hundred times, and I did, until there were no more bullets, and it was too dark to see, until I could hold the gun without trembling, fire it without thinking. Until I remembered to say Doba's name each time I shot.

But my thoughts were on the last thing I'd read in the book, the last thing Davey had said about promising to kill him, that he didn't want to live like he was.

At eleven forty-five, we sat in the kitchen and Cade loaded the gun. We turned off the lights in the house, so my eyes could grow accustomed to the dark like a preda-tor's would, like those of the animal I would shoot.

Sitting silently across from each other, we waited for the creature to come. And for Davey.

17

raine

The blue moon was full and bright, shining through Cade's kitchen windows, bathing everything in light. It seemed an omen, this brightness. No more lies. No more secrets. Nowhere else to hide.

The better to see you with, my dear.

Those lines from Little Red Riding Hood popped into my head, and I remembered how Davey would bug his eyes and giggle when I'd read them, me the wolf, him Little Red Riding Hood for just that instant.

I was the hunter tonight.

I'd asked Luna earlier why she thought it had gone to Cade's home instead of ours when it searched for Davey. Maybe it was because of that white ash I spread around, she'd said. It wouldn't bother it in human form, Doba had come into the yard without any fear, but after it shifted, the ash would have kept it away, not kill it, just make it wary. It had killed Dennie in Cade's home—gone there in both human and animal form, so it knew the surroundings, and like all beasts of prey, it liked to kill in familiar surroundings. Davey must have known that, too. The white ash may have kept him from coming home after he'd shifted. But I didn't want to think about that now.

Some things are impossible to face. They can kill you.

I remembered the words I'd said to Cade that day in Starbucks, and silently I repeated his words to me.

Not if you kill it first. Not if you kill it first. Not if you kill it first.

"You okay?" Cade whispered, bringing me back. I nodded that I was. Surprise would be the best way to shoot it, we'd decided. The moment we heard it break into Dennie's office, I'd go in and shoot immediately, not give it time to think, attack, or shift—because it certainly would. There were three bullets in the gun, and any one of them could kill it—as long as I said its name.

But was I sure of its name?

"Raine, I need to tell you something." Cade's voice was strained and tense. He was as afraid as I was, and yet he stayed with me. "You know how I feel about you, right?"

I nodded, my throat too tight to answer.

"I just wanted you to know, before . . ." He didn't need to finish, because we both knew what would happen. If this didn't work, it would kill all three of us the same way it had killed Dennie and Mack, without thought or mercy.

The growl came loud and deep from outside the house. I closed my eyes, steadying myself, holding my breath.

Slow down, Mom. Slow down, Mom. Take a breath.

"Davey." Saying his name helped me push the air from the pit of my stomach through my chest and from my lips.

A shimmering crash of shattered glass was followed by a growl and a moan as it crashed through the office window; then came the mewling whine of another animal, something small and in trouble, something as frightened as I was. I was only conscious of my stomach squeezing so hard, I thought I would be sick—of my heart beating so loud, I thought it might hear me. Davey was in that room, too.

"He's come here to draw it to him," Cade whispered in a voice heavy with fear. "I was afraid he might do that. He must have come in when I was out. I should have checked the room when I came back. I'm sorry, Raine. I should have—" He stopped short, and we sat motionless, listening to the sound of something being thrown against the wall followed by the high-pitched squeal of a wounded animal.

Cade reached for the gun. "Let me do it, Raine. I know how to shoot, I've done it before. Let me shoot the goddamn thing before it's too late."

"It's for me to do, not you," I said. Davey was mine. I had to face down what wanted to kill him. It was my life that should be risked, not Cade's. I picked up the gun that lay between us, my palms sweating so hard, I was sure I would drop it, but I held it tight, too tightly. I tried to loosen my grip, like Cade had told me to do, almost like you're shaking hands, he'd said, but I couldn't do it. I counted instead—one, two, three, four—and tried to relax each muscle in my hand as I remembered how my grandfather would count for me before I aimed his gun.

In a dream state, I stepped away from Cade in slow motion into that room, hardly feeling the door as I opened and closed it behind me, knowing I had to keep in whatever wanted to get out. Breathe like Davey tells you to, I said to myself—then hold it light, aim, shoot, anywhere it hits will be good, but don't forget to say its name. Don't forget to say its name.

If you know its name.

I saw only broken glass at first, shining in a pool of jagged edges, then its eyes, narrow and amber, gleaming like a tiger's from a far corner of the room. It was tall, standing on two legs. What form had it taken? How much of what was human lingered inside? Did it know I was here to kill it?

Where was Davey?

I wanted to scream the words out, like I did in the church that time, to feel his presence like I had before. Yet I knew he was something else now. A Davey I didn't know, had never seen. Was he hiding from it? From me? Had it wounded him? Killed him?

I braced myself against the door, stealing strength and calm from its hard, smooth surface. I waited for it to lunge before I shot, to make its move before I did.

"Davey! Come to me. I want to see you," it said.

Nothing within me moved—not my breath, my heart, or the hand that held the gun.

"Wherever you are, Davey, come out so I can see you, so I can hug you once again."

It had taken my voice. It would use it to kill my son.

Something soft and furry rubbed up against my leg like a small dog or large cat does, and licked me with its rough tongue. I stooped down and touched his head, not sure what animal he had become, hoping my touch would tell him I was here, let him know who I was, that those words weren't mine.

"Davey," it said again. "I'm over here next to the desk. Come here now!" It stunned me to hear my own voice, angry and demanding, commanding him from across the room.

But it had told me where it was.

Three bullets. Three chances.

I stooped again, feeling around in the dark for the soft, curly hair of his animal back, but he wasn't there. Had he gone, run to what called him?

I won't be small like that again, like I was in church today. Never. I'm through with it.

But he was still small. He'd come up only to my knee, not nearly so strong or big as he needed to be. He wasn't ready, even though he thought he was.

"No," I said, not realizing I'd spoken aloud until the word was said. It came toward us, meeting Davey halfway, its gait rambling and uneven. It was unsure of itself on two legs; it killed better on four. Had this been the thing Dennie saw before it tore her apart? And Mack, thinking it was human until it showed its other side? I had to see it for myself, to know where to aim so I would shoot it and not my son. The light switch was on the wall near where I stood. I felt for it, turning it on, bathing the room in light. Startled, it looked toward me, momentarily blinded.

There was no biker or dowdy woman with lace gloves this time. No old woman in soiled black raincoat, wearing garish makeup to hide what was there. It was Anna, dressed as Luna had described Doba that day she came to find us.

The resemblance was striking, as it must always have

been between the cousins—so close, they could be mistaken for twins. Same steel gray hair, skin as smooth and
brown as leather, black bright eyes. But the hands were
the paws of a wolf. I could see Davey now, too, what he
had become. A wolf cub not yet grown with gray fur and
dark eyes like those of his grandmother, and I remembered the first time I saw Anna shift, when I had run away
to hide from what she was.

"Doba!" I screamed, stepping from the door, aiming,
firing. I heard the ping of the bullet as it cracked the side
of Dennie's desk, missing her by a foot.

It turned in my direction, ambled toward me with halt-
ing steps, unafraid and vicious, bearing the pointed teeth
of the old homeless woman, yet it had Anna's eyes filled
with the pleading light that was often in them when she
gazed at me, the look that showed how much she loved
us. I thought of how she'd tried to warn us about them—
the family that was bound to her.

*They gain power by committing an act of horror. Often it
is the murder of a blood relative.*

Anna's child. My Elan.

I fired again, the memory of what she'd done to Elan
squeezing the trigger, realizing too late I'd forgotten to
call its name.

"Davey!" it said in Anna's voice, calling him as she had
when she would fry bread for him in her kitchen, a voice
as sticky sweet as the sugar candy he loved. "Come to me,
my Davey. Let me see you as you are now. How grown
and fierce you are."

And Davey trotted toward her, an obedient child,
head held high in anticipation. It stooped gracefully, as if

to deliver a treat, then grabbed him fiercely by the neck, squeezing, shaking, then tossing him to the floor. He hit it with a squeaky, tremulous cry and then scrambled away, paws scraping the floor. It howled deep from within its animal throat, a final, triumphant killing sound.

Who guided my hand this time? Was it Anna, Mack, Elan? I aimed straight and shot clean, screaming its name as I did, then watched with horror and fascination as it began to change. Anna's face stretching into the wolf, shrinking into that of Doba. Arms and legs pulling themselves into those of a woman; its torso slowly taking human shape. Yet the paws remained the same, even as she shifted. Doba's thumb-less hand, Anna's ring still tight upon a finger.

In the silence, I could hear only one breath, my own. Davey lay where she had thrown him. He stared at me with eyes that didn't belong to him, those of a frightened orphaned cub who had witnessed the death of a loved protector, a member of his pack. He had heard her voice, Anna's voice, and he had seen her change before his eyes. Doba was blood, as Anna was, and the blood that had captured him flowed deep. I was their killer.

Whose was he now? Hers or mine?

And if it kills me, I don't care. I'd rather die than live like the kind of freak I am. Kill me if it doesn't.

He limped across the room, still wounded, and stopped at Doba's body, touching it with his nose, sniffing it, licking it with his small, rough tongue, and my heart squeezed tight because he was my son. His animal eyes took me in, head leaning to one side as an animal does before it attacks, pondering how to kill. He moved toward me, then warily circled me in that tight room, baring his fangs, a growl, her growl, coming from deep within his throat.

"Say my name," I said to him. "Say my name."

He tipped his head to one side, as if he couldn't quite hear, a glimmer of curiosity in his eyes. I wondered if he was listening as he always did to another voice, another sound that had always been closed to me.

"Say it, Davey. Say it!" I screamed, ordering him like I had throughout his life: Eat your vegetables. Say your prayers. Get ready for bed. Do your homework. Stay inside. Listen to me when I speak to you. "Goddamn it, Davey, say my name! Say it now. Now!"

It snarled, slow and sharp. A growl, not word, not name.

If the creature remains unchanged, its evil runs too deep and it will die.

"Say Raine!" I screamed, begging to hear something in that sound, just underneath it.

"Rrrrrr." Was he trying to say it, form it with this animal mouth of his? Was I imagining it? He moved closer to me, head bowed.

"Again, again, again!" I screamed like I did when we would go through his multiplication tables. Listen to me. Say them again, again, and again.

"Rrrainne."

I knelt down to his level, grabbed his round soft head, and held it in my hands, not afraid of him anymore.

"Raine," I said. "Raine. Raine. Raine."

I thought about that time in church, my annoyance, me scolding him because he called me by my name, not Mom, and tears came into my eyes. If I could hear him say my name once more, just once before I died. Before he did.

"Raaaiinnee." It came out low, buried somewhere from within him. "Raine!"

He changed as Doba had, bit by bit, each animal part transformed into human. Legs, arms, torso, and finally his face until he lay beside me, the son I knew and loved.

"Mom!" he said, crying as hard as I was.

We sat at Cade's kitchen table, the four of us. Too tired to think or talk. Davey had put on a pair of Cade's gray sweats and was finishing off his second glass of apple juice. I watched him, loving him more than I ever thought I could.

After a time, Luna spoke. "So how do you feel?"

"Okay." He was a kid again, not saying more than he had to.

"What do you remember?" she said, and he gazed at me, knowing we shared a secret that neither of us would ever tell.

"Not much."

"Want some more juice?" Cade asked.

"Sure."

Cade went to the refrigerator, poured out another glass, and handed it to him. "Took a lot out of you, huh?"

Davey shrugged. "Not much." He gulped down the glass and handed it back to Cade for a refill, which was promptly given.

"You sure you're okay, Davey?" I asked after a minute.

Davey looked at me, his head cocked to the side. "Hey, you think you can call me something else now? Davey's a kid's name."

"Like what?"

"I don't know, Mom. Maybe D or King D or . . . Wolf," he said with a twinkle in his eye. "Something cool like that."

"Wolf?" I asked, unbelieving.

"Not a great idea," Cade said. "How about just . . . Dave?"

"That'll do," he said with a shrug, and for the first time in a week, we all laughed.